THE LOKI ADVENTURES

DIAL UP MISCHIEF IF YOU DARE

PERFECT 10

A LOKI ADVENTURE

DAWN BLAIR

MORNING SKY STUDIOS

CHAPTER 1

Click. Click. Click. Click. Click.

The staccato sound of my black stiletto heels on the smooth sidewalk keeps the steady time of my elegant pace as I stride confidently toward the austere industrial building. The exterior is covered in flat metal painted in grey-blue and white, giving it not only a plain appearance, but cold as well. The designer tried to give it some flow and movement in painting a cool, demure blue at an angle across the building, but it reminds me of a spear buried tip upward in the snow and leaves me feeling shallow and unforgiving.

Probably a good thing considering I'm going in to close a case.

The company knows I'm coming. Jason, my personal assistant, set up the appointment yesterday. The transdimensional being who has been naughty on earth and works for the company does not know that I am on my way. I love it when they never see me coming.

A light dusting of snow decorates the early spring grass. It's all cut to a level height indicating that someone did some lawn care recently. Leave it to the weather to prove that good temperatures are not quite here yet. In another era, some people might even blame me, Loki of Asgard, for such inclement conditions, and ordinarily they would not be wrong. I do like playing Jack Frost come to nip at your nose and fingertips.

But not this year.

Right now, I have too many cases and they seem to be steadily on the rise. It's really quite hard to be carefree and pleasure-loving when you're just flat-out overworked. To be doing all this in a short black skirt and heels makes it all that much worse. The hair appointments, the manicures, and the pedicures, are just all too much to fit into a schedule like mine.

But, to look this fantastic as a woman here on Midgard, I must do what I must do. Do not ever say that Loki of Asgard skimps on his (or her) appearance.

I could use an illusion for all the glamor, and that would be simple enough. Even when Odin had my powers locked down while I was on parole here on Midgard, I could do at least that much. Now, the All-Father doesn't realize that I've been given a substantial amount of my power back. I'd like to keep it that way.

Besides, I do like to look pretty and to turn heads. There's just something about that power. The right sidelong look from soft bedroom eyes, a coy smile given with a suggestive tilt of the head. Oh, to hear the heartbeats quicken. That is fantastic.

But now is not that time. I shake the wishful longing from my shoulders and remind myself what I am here to do. A transdimensional being -- probably escaped from a terrible life in their home dimension, but couldn't appreciate what they had, is trying to make Midgard into their world. Why do people move away from conditions they don't like only to try to recreate them in the new place? I used to think it was only humans that could be so contradictory, but of late, I see that the multidimensional universe is filled with such illogical creatures.

All of it is just as irrational as believing that someone who is beautiful or handsome on the outside is as put together and fantastic on the inside. A perfect ten can be a complete miserable and horrific dud with their personality.

A little office section of the building sticks out a ways from the rest of the sterile metal building. Beneath the sloping metal roof are big windows. Through the glass, I see a woman sitting at a desk, phone up to her ear. She's smiling and laughing with whoever she's talking to.

I'm about to ruin her day.

It makes me feel half bad, I tell you. Oh, in the overall scheme of things, she'll not remember anything. I'll take her memories of the events, but until I do that, she's going to be very unhappy. Possibly a little (or a lot) scared if things get out of control. Hmm.

I reach for the metal –shocker!—handle of the office's glass door. The cold bar stretches straight across the full width of the door. A grey metal frame holds the tempered glass. As I draw the door open, I hear the insulating foam around the door and under the sweep whisper as if its hushing me to silence as I enter the quiet office. Even the woman chatting on the phone is almost noiseless.

The hairs, gorgeous brown that it is, at the back of my neck starts to raise.

The office has the faint scent of wood cleaner and oily mechanics. Not surprising since the receptionist's desk is wood and this is an industrial building where they use a lot of machines in making something. Jason had informed me what they do here. I think they were manufacturing screws and bolts, everything from common household hardware to specialty and custom fasteners. I guess someone has to do it.

I realize why the woman had gone silent. Just as I'd seen her, she'd noticed me as I approached the building and excused herself from the conversation. The cell phone currently lay face down on her desk. An ordinary human wouldn't have been able to tell if the phone was still connected to the other person. Thank goodness I'm neither ordinary nor human. The line is still engaged and the person on the other end capable of hearing everything I say. I now regret not calling to disable the phones here. Sloppy, Loki, very sloppy.

"Can I help you?" the receptionist asks, her voice bright.

I find this strange. Typically, when a female of Midgard encounters me for the first time, there is a natural tendency for the other woman to be reserved and cool toward me. They seem to know that something is off, one of the reasons I prefer my male form here on Midgard. I can get a better initial reaction out of men or women that way. But, since I'm stuck in my female form for the moment, for reasons I have yet to understand, I expected this conversation to already start out differently.

I look at the woman a bit closer, observing her more closely now, with a more discerning eye, you might say.

She is not your "motherly type." There are just some women who one looks at and you just know they are a mother. Whether they are a good one or not is another question entirely. Now this receptionist is a few years shy of truly taking on such a look, but generally there is something in the eyes that indicates this appearance will come.

She's not the "stern and jaded by life" either. That classic look seems to be reserved for politicians. This woman has no hope of ever even running for a city council.

Yet she's also not the "sensual kitten" either. Oh, she's pretty with her light brown hair that falls softly about her shoulders, the sides pulled back in a pony tail. She wears her makeup too lightly and it lets her natural beauty shine through. Still, she's rather plain overall.

But there's something…

I know I must say something. She's sitting there looking at me expectantly, smile still wide and waiting on her face. But the cheerfulness is a mask. It's a little spot in her eyes that tells me that. It's as if she can see through my deception.

Fear sparkles through me.

I have never felt this way. Why now? What has she done? Who is she? Is she a transdimensional?

Each of these questions rushes in like biting raptors to latch onto my thoughts.

I barely notice her stand.

I am weighed down, unable to think.

"Don't worry," she says cooly. "I know why you're here. We all do."

CHAPTER 2

I pull from the warm, dark embrace of the fabric of Midgard, surfacing like a ball held under the surface of water. With a gasp, I open my eyes and find Midgard brilliantly lit.

The white shining all around me is too much and I hiss in pain. Closing my eyes and trying to turn my head from the radiance of the sun pouring down on me, I realize my hands are tried down straight out from me. I don't know if my feet are tied as well, but they don't appear to be as I bring a knee up in my attempt to shield my body from the sun and light.

Going fetal, I realize to my dismayed horror.

Gods do not feel fear.

Yet something had struck me on such a primal level that I had. What was it?

My mind clicks back trying to find the last moment I remember. Yes, I'd gone to close a case and had been in an industrial building. Now, I lay on my back, sort of twisted and half curled up, arms pinned down as if I were being crucified on what feels and moves beneath me like desert sand.

Am I still in Midgard?

I try to sit up, needing desperately to look around. If I've been taken somewhere else… well, that wouldn't be good. Odin… he'd have to act as if I were breaking the parole that both he and I know I'm not longer under, but no other gods are aware of it.

The rope binding my wrists hold me firmly so that I can't edge up any more than how far my shoulders will flex. Not that it matters. My vision won't adjust from the harsh whiteness and everything is blurred as if I'm looking through frosted glass. Have I been dosed with something? Is that why I don't know how I've gotten out here?

If I'm off-Midgard, Jason won't even be able to track my phone to come aid me. I won't say "rescue" because certainly I will have myself out of this conundrum before Jason even knows I'm gone. Of course, that thought leads me to wondering just how long I have been out.

I test to see if my legs are staked down as well. They are, but the ropes aren't as tight and they give me some room to move.

There's a sagebrush, big and round, about three feet out from my right hip. It's starting to come into focus now. So, I am in the desert. Yet the ground beneath me is too sandy to be from the sagebrush steppe near where I live. Still, it gives me hope that I am in Midgard.

I hear a shuffling sound, like feet scurrying across the sand. I twist my head to see if I can locate the noise, but it stops as soon as the maker realizes I've heard the noise. Next time, I must remain motionless and not give myself away.

Then, I realize I'm in pants. This is my male form. Had I

shifted back while I was unconscious? No, I couldn't have. Changing my gender wouldn't change my clothes. I'd be a male in a very short black skirt and heels if that were the case.

I raise my head to look down my arms. Yes, I'm even in one of my jackets. This is one of my favorite suits and it's now getting ruined here in the desert sand. Now I'm bewildered, annoyed, and irked. Someone will pay dearly for this.

More shuffling, and it's really close. So close, in fact, that I whip my head toward the sound instinctually regardless of how I'd told myself that I needed to remain still.

The sagebrush stands right beside me, leaning over me, and starting at me with wide brown eyes amid a grey-green face. As I gasp, the sagebrush opens its mouth and laughs at me. It giggles even harder as I startle and half try to squirm away.

What the heck is going on with me?

"Ahh, eyes open and seeing, I see," the sagebrush says with a bright voice.

If I thought for one instance that I could have been drugged and feeling the affects, I'd assume I was hallucinating with a bad trip.

The sagebrush cocks its head and I realize that it isn't one mass, but more resembles a man crouched beside me. There's definitely knees tucked up beside its body, shoulders, and a head. What looks like the branches of a sagebrush is really the clothing that the man wears along with a matching headdress. Now that I've seen it, I wonder how I could have ever thought that it was a sagebrush to begin with. Optical illusions sure are strange.

"Ohh," it croons at me, leaning in a bit closer.

"What do you want?" I snapped the words and instantly regretted my mistake. The sagebrush man jumps back and half turns away. I fear that he's about to scuttle off. The ragged sticks of his outfit slowly quit shaking.

I use the moment to try to get my arms free. I can see the short stake that tethers the bonds to the ground. It doesn't seem like it would be hard to pull up if I can just get the right leverage on it.

The sagebrush rocks as the man turns back toward me. "I could let you up."

"A smart creature would have done that already, knowing that I'm going to be very angry when I do get free. Were you the one who put me here?"

"Shat'tow don't do that."

"Your name's Shat'tow?" I ask. "I'm Loki, Loki of Midgard. I presume you've heard of me?"

The sagebrush man smiles and I can tell that the grey-green appearance of his face is caused by paint. It cracks a little in the wrinkles around his eyes and I can tell that he has a darker complexion beneath. "Don't matter who you are. You stuck to the ground."

As if to emphasize his words and mock me further, he reaches out a hand and points with a downward curved index finger. Like salt in my wounds, he chuckles again.

Shat'tow is really starting to annoy me.

"How about we fix that?" I ask. Then, with a layer of enchantment over my words, I say, "You want to release me."

"Tsk, tsk, tsk. That don't work here," Shat'tow says, still chuckling.

"Money? How about money? I'll pay you to let me up." A thought strikes me as I suddenly wonder if he's a type of desert fairy. "If you like shiny, I've got lots of sparkly coins. I'll give you some."

"Tsk, tsk, tsk, tsk, tsk. That don't work here either."

I am quickly tiring of this game. "What do you want then?"

I have too many cases right now and no time for this. I don't see how my predicament could be related to any of my cases either, unless someone has hired the weird little sagebrush man to stall me, bind me, or assassinate me. Other than really annoying me, I don't know how Shat'tow could really harm me. But everybody has a price, and I will find Shat'tow's. Then I will find out what's really going on here and who is behind this. I might be overworked, but I think I can find some extra wrath to deal out some vengeance for this.

"Loki has nothing I want," Shat'tow says.

"I find that hard to believe. Everyone wants something. What do you want?"

"Nothing. There is nothing Shat'tow wants. Sun shines down on me, gives me everything I need. Sun tells me if I live… or die. Sun good and sun dangerous. Without sun, nothing exist. So, Shat'tow have all needs met by the sun. But don't worry. I know why you're here," Shat'tow says. "We all do."

CHAPTER 3

I t felt like the weight of the world was on me.

Literally.

I still lay on my back as I start to wake up as my eyes began to flutter open, but now something heavy sits in my chest. No, it was definitely on my chest rather than being inside my ribcage. It's a good thing that I don't actually need to breathe.

My chest is also the only part of me that feels warm.

Ordinarily, I'd be grateful for the cold. But, if I were still out in the desert, I'd still be warm all over. I've moved… teleported… or whatever this is, once again. If I open my eyes, will it still be bright?

Unsure, I squint, barely opening my eyes but the tiniest amount.

"Papa!" Fenrir says. Then he begins to lick my face.

But he's not puppy Fenrir. He's in hellhound form, sitting on my chest with his legs straddling me, and slobbers all over my face with a scruffy, muscular tongue.

"Fen, get off," I say.

The response I get is him lowering his head right on top of mine. I barely have time to turn my face away. I feel my chin against his neck, a strange sensation going through my teeth as he starts to growl.

"Not now, Papa," he says between growls.

A whistle sounds overhead, going from the left side of me above my head to the right side off by my feet somewhere, followed by an explosion which shakes through the ground. There's heavy mechanical footsteps getting closer. I hear gears turning, then smashing. Whaaa-pauk. Whaaa-pauk.

"Fen!"

My face is so buried in his fur that the word is completely muffled. If I'm lucky, the hellhound felt the vibration of me speaking, though he certainly doesn't show any indication of me speaking his name. Fenrir's grey skin is rough and wrinkly, not unlike an elephant, even with the short, sparse, and wiry hairs. Certainly not the fluffy puppy I'm used to. He even carries with him the scent of earth and smoke.

More crashes around us and I realize that Fenrir is protecting me from whatever is around us.

"Battle, Papa," he says as if he can read my thoughts. He might be able to.

But, he forgets that I'm a god and he isn't quite. He's fallible.

I reach my hand up, stretching a little so that I can grab the scruff of his neck and pull him off me. He growls his displeasure, but removes himself from me at my insistent urging. I take a paw to the stomach as he moves over me. I'm pretending it wasn't intentional, but I have a feeling it was. Once Fenrir is no longer protectively covering me, he still takes a stance with his legs apart to guard me.

I swear what is going on around me is Ragnarök. Dust

hangs like fog in the air and darkens the landscape to grey, lightening only where the sun's rays try to penetrate through. There are huge mechanical vehicles crawling over the landscape. It is their tread complete with spiked plates that had made the weird sounds I'd heard moments before. The ground churns as the plates tear from the earth and churn up soil.

I try to tell who is battling, but I only see vague dark silhouettes of humanoids moving in the thick dust.

"What's going on?" I ask Fenrir.

"Battle, Papa," he repeats.

Ah, the young stating the obvious. But in battle, no one is ever right or wrong. It is the old asking the youthful to fight a battle the old no longer can. It is death come in the name of continuing a certain way of life. Yet at the core, there is always an intruder who has come to foreign soil.

"Fen," I say, laying my hand on Fenrir's bony shoulder blade, "Take us to the ones who call this their territory."

For too long of a moment, we remain where we stand. Missiles whiz overhead and shatter behind us. The repeated pinging of gunfire sounds in the distance.

"We're not going, Papa." The frustration is evident in Fenrir's voice. "You are the one that is wronged. This is your territory, your hall on Midgard."

Right. I had left Fenrir at home. Where else would he be?

I take another swinging look around and begin to see the familiar. The house, shrouded though it is in the grey cloud of dirt hanging in the air, still stands protected by my enchantments. There's a momentary clutch of anxiety as I wondering if someone is trying to get to the totems in my basement. I have a lot of cases going. I'm sure I've mentioned that I'm overworked at the moment. But the house is sound and no one seems particularly interested in trying to breech my security.

There's the tree Fenrir lies to lay under. Now that's another story. It's been uprooted and split in two. Huge chunks of it lay scattered. It'd say that it had been victim to a missile and to the plated vehicles rolling over everything.

Beneath my feet – I don't want to look – oh, there it is and it is as terrible as I imagined it would be, the remains of my brick driveway. I stand on (and had been lying on) the only intact piece of it. Everything else is broken and torn.

Well, if my neighbors didn't think I was strange before, they certainly are going to wonder what I'm up to now. I'm sure I'll get a dust complaint from all the farmers around me, not like they never plow their fields or anything. I'm not even going to go into my conspiracy theories of how they all plot and plan to do their field work when the wind is blowing right toward my house.

Well, now what?

"All right, Fen, take me to the leader of the heathens doing this," I say.

He teleports us.

Right away, things change in the silence which falls around us. Firstly, I'm back to being a woman and trip awkwardly on the slick marble floor as one heels slides inward toward the other, rolling my ankle a bit. I've never known shoes to tremble in fear, but I feel that is exactly what just happened. Secondly, I am in a expansive, grand hall complete with Grecian marble columns and hieroglyphics on the golden walls, and everyone else in the room falls silent.

"Ah, Loki. About time," a woman's voice rings out from among the mass of females huddled around her. "I hope you know why you're here."

CHAPTER 4

Aside from me once again being back in female form, I notice instantly that Fenrir is back to being a puppy. The other women in the room, about a dozen or so of them, begin to coo over his cuteness, to which he tilts his head and lets the tip of one of his ears flop over. He loves being the charmer.

Gee, I wonder where he gets that from.

And, I realize, that it's a good thing I'm a woman myself right now as these are not females who would be charmed by any male who wasn't cute and fluffy.

I stand in the hall of the Amazons.

This is not at all like the place ruled by Queen Aleincia, which makes me wonder if this is another tribe, or perhaps a different time. Or considering that the women still remark over Fenrir, not seeing his true hellhound form, I might not even be in a true Amazonian hall. Figuring out either option is difficult at the moment. I must take in more clues.

I find it very hard to believe that the mechanical devices

wreaking havoc on my house and home were sent by the Amazons. "Are you sure you brought us to the right place?" I ask Fenrir. "Is your scenting ability off?"

Fenrir gives me a gesture as akin to a shrug as he can possibly manage, then resumes looking cute for the women around him.

The expansive room smells of smoke, cinnamon, and rosemary. What I initially thought were hieroglyphics on the walls I now see are neither Egyptian in origin nor quite Aztec symbols. They could, in fact, be older, as are the supposed Grecian columns, these ones representing a Mediterranean style are broken up into three sections and pre-date the rise of Greek architecture.

No togas there, and I still wear the same stylish outfit I'd put on earlier in my day. The women all wear similar cuts in their outfits, but different types of soft, flowing materials. Each is a halter top and loose leggings which resemble more skirts than pants. The latter varies in length though, from shorts, to knee-length, to all the way down to the ankles. The halter tops cover more than it exposes and from the few I can see from the side, the style crosses the back so the shirt won't shift while working or battling. Practical and efficient.

A cluster of seven sun-kissed women sit on a slightly raised platform. The area is big enough that they could easily sit in a circle, but there chairs are currently spread in a semi-arch so that they can watch the participants who stand on the floor nearest me. Many of the standing women hold quarter staves or wooden swords in their hands. Nearly every one of them has a pistol holstered at their side or tucked into the small of their back. Practicing the old warfare, if I had to guess, but preparing for the new.

All the women in the not-quite-straight line on the small

riser are looking at me, but I figure the one in the center is the leader. Her eyes are particularly dark and lined with kohl. Gold flecks dust her espresso-toned face. Her supple lips take on a slight upturn as she watches me assessing her. Outwardly, I may look female at the moment, but gender doesn't stop me from appreciating her swart beauty. There's a small part of me that nudges to remind myself that I am not a man. At least, not a typical man.

Not that the Amazons – if this even is a different tribe of Amazons -- are against men, necessarily, as they have always been portrayed. We both know that mythology has roots in truth, but is often overblown by storytellers needing to hold an audience. Even still, kernel of truth, and I should not hold myself among the mortals of Midgard.

I am a god.

A god, apparently stuck – except during whatever the last couple side trips were about – in a female appearance.

I square my shoulders and raise my chin just a touch. She is still waiting for my answer and not about to repeat herself.

"Apologies, my luscious queen," I say with a half bow, half curtsey. Her name comes to me, rippled as if on call through the fabric of Midgard – Rhetallia. As fantastic and unusual as I suspect that she is. I also realize that I have done her a disservice in calling her queen, for that implies that there is a king. The Amazons – or this group, whatever they are -- have modernized in this era. "I do not know why I am here, Leader Rhetallia."

The woman beside Rhetallia leans over and whispers something, but Rhetallia dismisses her with a wave of her hand.

"Do you not, my dear Loki of Midgard, have in your possession a spear?"

Well, Rhetallia knew I was "of Midgard" now, so a backward time jump seemed unlikely. Forward, still quite probable. But how likely was it that the entire hall of the Amazons had been redecorated? I very much doubt it. So, it seems like another tribe of Amazons is my answer. Queen Aleincia had said that it would be a sister asking for a favor; she didn't say it would be one directly of her own.

Again, she is waiting for my answer and will not be repeating herself.

"I have many things," I say, trying to keep my mind focused away from the odd assortment of items locked away in my basement. I don't know if one of these dark, lovely ladies might have the sort of perception which picks up on another's thoughts. "You will have to be a little more specific and describe this spear."

The woman beside Rhetallia whispers again, and this time Rhetallia nods to her. As if she'd been dismissed from the dinner table, the woman slides off her chair and takes a quick pace out of the room through a side door.

Rhetallia glances back at me. "Onya reminds me that you would know the spear if you had seen it. Therefore, we must acknowledge that it is not in your possession yet."

There is a lot hanging on that last word: yet.

However, there is one simple fact about my life right now. "Leader Rhetallia, I must beg your pardon at this time, but I cannot go on a quest for you." I held my arms out to the side as if I was giving an innocent, but pleading shrug.

I expect to see her expression harden and become stern. Leaders are typically used to getting their way and don't like it when someone tells them no. However, her face remains supple and soft, eyes full of understanding. I'm afraid for a moment that she really isn't taking my meaning.

"I specialize in sending transdimensional beings back to their home worlds and right now I have far too many cases of tracking down these creatures to be taking on any side work," I tell her. "Unfortunately, I must remain loyal to the work I have now. When it dies down, I shall be more than happy to help you find this spear."

"That doesn't work for us," Rhetallia says. "I am afraid that we must speed things along."

I can tell I'm going to have to be more insistent and strong about this. "I really do not have the time. I have thirty cases –"

A ripple goes through the fabric of Midgard as if it is laughing at me at the same time the side door opens. Amid the dark, there is a sudden ray of blonde light and my heart skips a beat before I even fully realize who has just entered the room. A Valkyrie, but not just any of the Asgardian angels, but a fallen Valkyrie. Who better to become a sister to the Amazons?

Pulse racing, I take a sidelong glance. It is not enough. I turn my head.

It is true.

Alongside Onya walks a Valkyrie in an outfit similar to the others in the room, save the sword at her side is very real and sharp. She might as well as wings for my own heart takes flight.

It is Becca.

CHAPTER 5

Becca, the fallen Valkyrie once known as Gelsh, walks into the room and I feel as if my entire life comes to a standstill.

She is as beautiful as she was when I first met her on the college campus, before I knew who and what she really was, and she was just my most current case. Her blonde hair is curled and fluffy, and shines like a radiant sun. Her spirit is as strong-willed as it was the day I stood outside her mother's daycare after Fenrir had "escaped" and we had that regretful fight.

Her outfit is the same as the other women's, but she is in the shorts version of it. The dusty rose color suits her complexion well and makes her eyes seem even bluer. Her forehead glistens with perspiration, but there is a trail of sweat downing down alongside her face. It looks like she wiped the droplet away before enter the room as her skin still shows the reddened indication of the smudge of her palm against her cheek.

Becca stops beside her Amazonian sister and looks me over.

Does she have any clue who I am… really? Does she see me as the Loki she knows? Or does she see me as a stranger?

Instantly, I feel cold all over.

The room, as expansive and ornate as it is, suddenly takes on an oppressive feel. The walls seem to close in, arching over me as if I'm a child huddled under a blanket too afraid to face the monsters of the dark. I feel blackness creeping in at the edges of my vision. Dear Odin, break me out of this.

As a Valkyrie, Becca would have seen right through the feminine illusion around me, but as a mere mortal, she only sees another woman. Unless one of the Amazons told her, she would have no reason to believe that I am the same Loki she knows. And even then, who would believe such a far-fetched story such as a person changing their sex.

Except that we are living in a new age of Midgard.

I'm sure the unbidden thought was sent to comfort me, but I certainly don't take it that way. Even if she does think that I was just a pretty boy who underwent an operation to become a woman, the moment I transform back will leave her with distinct impressions of me that her mind as a mortal might not be able to comprehend.

It could get very weird.

I must do something and it must be quick.

I break off an illusion of myself so that I can move quickly behind Rhetallia. I flow like smoke in hopes that I can go faster than anyone can see me go. Some might take it as an attack, especially if they know I am capable of doing this.

"Newest sister," Rhetallia begins, "I'd like to introduce you to –"

"Laufey," the illusion of me says very quickly. "You may call me Laufey."

Rhetallia's head swivels to give the illusion of me a strange look, and when she does, she startles to notice me leaning in at her shoulder.

"Follow my lead," I whisper to her, "or this spear you are looking for will never appear on Midgard again. Understand?"

Rhetallia gives a small nod as she finishes, "—Laufey. She has come to help us in our quest."

Satisfied that Rhetallia understands my desire to be called by my mother's name, I resume the spot where my illusion had been standing as if I'd never left. "Potentially help. I have not agreed yet, though it certainly has been made more tempting."

"I do believe, my dear Laufey, that you have given me more leverage than you realize. Besides, you have no right to refuse me," Rhetallia says. "We did your bidding and a favor was granted in return. I come to you now and request that you fulfill that favor. Please do not make me demand it."

Damn, she is right. She now has more persuasive ability that I'd like her have and she can hang it over my head like blackmail. She knows that I don't want Becca to know that I am Loki, and Rhetallia can expose me if I don't play nicely. Fine mess you've gotten yourself into this time, Loki. Or should I say, Laufey? I suppose I should get used to my mother's name. I may have just set a dangerous precedence here.

All right. Since I have placed myself in this predicament, I might as well begin to work to get myself out of it. Take the case and treat it like any other.

Becca walks toward me and the action makes me lose any emotional detachment I wish to have. Can she see the sorrow and worry in my eyes? Does she see right through the outer façade to my immortal soul?

Again, I am overcome by cold and goose bumps raise down my arms.

Becca stops before more and raises her eyes to mine. In the heels, I am a good four inches taller than her. It makes me wonder if my height has changed when I take the feminine form. Hmm. Odd to be noticing that now as I find me wanting to lose myself in the sky blue depths of her gaze.

There is a white feather subtly braided into the under layers of her hair.

I had neither noticed the braid nor the feather until she stood before me, and now that I have noticed it, I realize it is not a normal feather, but one quite magical.

Beyond a doubt, it is a Valkyrie feather.

"I am glad you have come to help," Becca says.

"Just returning a favor," I say. I must gain some distance. With that in mind, I look back toward Rhetallia. "Tell me what you know about this spear."

"Becca, do you wish to tell Laufey, or shall I?" Rhetallia asked.

Becca's shoulders straightened. "The spear was under my guard. I was to protect it, and I failed. It was stolen and has now been cast away where I cannot get it."

Her voice tried to sound so strong, but I could tell this event hurt her deeply. She'd been emotionally shamed and felt guilty. Since she went by the name *Becca*, I doubted that her Valkyrie memories had been awoken, but perhaps the feather in her hair made her carry the deep emotions of Odin's angels. I had to wonder how she'd come to be with the Amazons. Considering that she'd been happily living a mortal life, this had to be an odd turn. I wonder if she'd felt like I had as I'd been bounced between worlds to get here.

I chide myself for my curiosity. I must make this a case no

different than any other. Yet, I wonder why so many of them have come back around to have her in them. What is Midgard doing?

No time for that now. It's a case. One of one too many that I have. I certainly don't have time to indulge myself in questions.

"Who stole the spear and what did they do with it?" I ask.

"It has been embedded in a comet bound for Earth," Becca said.

Well, that explained why it was out of her reach.

"And the person who put it there?"

Her eyes narrow, taking on an angry head. "The god known as Thor."

CHAPTER 6

I am about to laugh about my brother being at the heart of this when I realize that I am no longer in hall of the Amazonia leader, Rhetallia. Instead, I stand in the office of the industrial building where I'd been going to finish up my latest case.

The brunette secretary is coming around her desk now, muttering something about, "Right this way," while I feel as if I've lost the last few seconds of the conversation. I have, and they seem like a crucial few seconds.

As she rounds behind me and I catch her faint vanilla scent, I wonder if I am to follow her. As the wood cleaner and oiled mechanic scent comes back, I decide that I'd rather remain within her vanilla aroma and take to step behind her. I do certainly hope it had been her intention for me to follow and that she hadn't really been asking me to have a seat. Since she never looks back at me with a questioning look, I must presume that I am all right in my actions.

She leads me into a hallway with three closed doors on

each side and a final door at the end. The only difference between them all is that the ones going to the side are wood and the last one is metal and secured with a keypad. She takes a key from her pocket and opens the middle door to the right.

"This will be your office," she says as she hands me the key, which I take more out of confused instinct than conscious awareness. She turns on the light and steps aside, grinning at me as if I should be flattered because I've been given a desk.

"We have a half an hour lunch," she tells me. "I hope you don't mind going at twelve thirty. I like to go at noon, and the prior bookkeeper would always wait until I got back so that we could keep the office open during that time. Will that be all right with you?"

So, she believes I've been hired to do bookkeeping work? What about me would possibly give off that image? My shoes alone should scream that I don't work for a petty hourly wage. I'd be willing to bet they are nearly twice what this woman makes at her cushy job of answering the phone. All right, all right, simmer down, Loki. If I played my cards right, I might be able to get passed that keypad into the shop area without having to use magic. No one can catch onto the little rouse I have with Odin now, not to mention that by my charm more of my powers have been unlocked. Snapping an occasional Valkyrie hair assures that the ploy remains intact.

"Lunch whenever will be fine with me. Eating is a nicety, not a requirement."

As I'd hoped, my words send a spark of envy through her. She's glaring as she glances me up and down. I can't help tipping my foot ever so slightly so that my heel comes up off the floor and accentuates my elegantly toned calf muscles. I'm sure that if there was more distance between us, she'd be muttering curses under her breath. Of course, that just makes me smile a little more broadly and I try to hide my amusement behind innocence.

"I'm told you already know your way around our system," she says, her time definitely cooler now. "Password for your computer is on the desk. Oh, and the boss said you'll have a meeting with him in ten minutes. I'll let him know you're here."

This is getting in a little over my head. Time to be direct. "I was hoping for a tour of the plant. I don't suppose you can show me around first before you give him a call?" Get in, erase their memories, and get out leaving no one the wiser that I was here. After all, I do have whatever this whole spear matter is with the Amazons; one case ready to take the place of another. So much for decreasing my workload.

"Away you go," she says, quite ready to dismiss me. "I'll let the boss know you're here."

I know my speed dial is quicker than hers and that I can have the lines disconnected before she can say, "Hello." However, something about this doesn't feel right. Who hires a new employee and just says, "Here's your computer. Cheerio!" Unless this person had worked for them before or at a different site, which seems to be the case here. If I believed it.

No, there is more going on here than meets the eye. Since this was the first place I started these odd jumps from, there is a plot at work. Besides, at first, the secretary had no clue who I was and now she makes statements as if she knows I'm returning. There's a good chance that she's in on this plot.

Was the odd sagebrush man meant to do me in? I wonder if he will be this *boss* I'm meeting with. Nothing more I can do other than get the computer running and see if I can find out the mastermind behind all this. Once I know who is running the show, I will be able to figure out why these jumps are occurring.

Clearly feeling as if she'd done her duty, the secretary walks away from me without another word and leaves me to head into the office. It has been cleaned recently, but then the door shut again so that the bleachy odors of cleaning supplies has settled in with the dank air. I leave the door open in hopes that I can get some fresh air in here. It really is a good thing that I don't need to breathe, another nicety.

That amuses me as I wonder what the receptionist's reaction to that would be.

Aside from a lack of ventilation in the room, there's also no windows. Without sunlight, the office has a natural dreariness to it. The only thing that would make it worse would be if it had dark wood paneling. Instead, the slightly textured walls have cream colored paint coating them. I don't think the brightest of white could deter the brown overcast to this room.

At least the desk isn't one of those metal ones from the 1970's with all sorts of dents and dings. That at least has been upgraded to one of faux wood, but the rest of the office with the metal filing cabinets has a dated feel. There are plastic paper trays here, two of them. One is empty and dusted. The other is two-thirds full of papers with a thick layer of dirt on them. Someone, at some point, had tried to straighten the papers out. They look like old invoices. The top few pages possess corners that are curled up slightly. They have been here and ignored for a long time. It makes me a little sad that no one has ever dealt with them. I take the tray of unimportant and forgotten papers and dump it into the garbage. The papers swoosh down into the metal bin with a thump and seem to startle the garbage liner into full awakeness as it accepts its burden.

I set the tray back down on top of the other. Now, I can settle myself into the aged office chair with a bit more ease.

While the desk was updated, the chair hadn't been. It is so ergonomically incorrect that it's no wonder that the elder generation now has such back issues now. I can spend fifteen minutes in this chair in order to find out what is going on, but I certainly couldn't be here for months, let alone years. If ever there was a frightening thought which could grip me, it's that one. I may be overworked, but I am grateful I am not caged to a chair – and certainly not this one.

Reaching for the power button, I power up the computer and listen as it hums to life. It's probably about as new as this desk and if the abandoned papers were any clue as to the state of the computer tower, I'm betting this beast will be slow. I hate to think of how it's poor circuitry might be fried when it finds its way out to the Internet and discovers how outdated it is. Will it ever be able to catch up to the updates?

Leaning back in the creaking chair, I close my eyes for a moment and lose myself to the hum.

CHAPTER 7

"Oooooommmmmmmmmmmmm."

Behind my closed eyelids, the world beyond brightens as the computer hum turns to meditative chant and I realize that I'm no longer where I had been. I am once again in pants too and tied down in the sand.

"Ooooooommmmmmmmmmmmmm."

I don't want to open my eyes. I don't want to see the sagebrush man – in my imagination, I see him squatting with his knees up close to his chest -- chanting beside me. Nope. Not going to do it. I'm just going to stay here, eyes closed, until I pop off to the next stop. That, if it follows a pattern, should put me back with the Amazons. And Becca.

I wiggle my shoulders a little to nestle down in the sand. Yes, I will wait.

"Ooooooommmmmmmmmmmmmmm," Shat'tow drones beside me.

The weird, little sagebrush man does not exist. I am not tied down and unable to move. Nope, I'm relaxing on a nice sandy beach. That's just the sound of the ocean I hear. Waves coming in, waves going out.

As the chant begins anew, my head swirls with the sound of it. I am tossed helplessly along with the hum as if I were being tackled by an ocean wave. The world spins and suddenly I am grateful for being tied down; it reinforces that the sensation is only in my head.

Sand slips inside the cuff of my pants and I feel it against my leg. I swear I hadn't moved. Which means, something is by my leg. Just what I need. Creepy crawlies in the desert usually are looking for something to kill. And if that really is a scorpion I suspect crawling inside, it's only a matter of time before it tries to sting me.

Won't it be in for a surprise?

I just wish we didn't have to go through this charade. Seriously. Wouldn't it be nice if sagebrush man would notice and take care of the problem instead of warbling on?

Maybe he's…

…calling them.

I kick out, waiting to feel the sting, jerk, and open my eyes. I pull against the tethers holding me. Shat'tow begins to laugh.

"Not funny," I say to him. I still don't know what was running around my leg, but it appears to be gone now or at least on the other side of the cloth.

"Shat'tow finds humor. Good belly laughs."

"Yes," I say, feeling a serpent rising within me, "I might find more humor in it if we could laugh together at someone else's expense. What do you say?"

I turn my gaze toward Shat'tow and give him an enchanting smile as I see the interest on his face. He's thinking about it.

"I know someone who would be a lot of fun to hold

down." That little thrilling tingle I feel in my stomach when I know that I'm coming up with a plan that's no good… yeah, I'm feeling it now. Could I trick Thor into my place? Oh, this is a devious plan, one that could get me into so much trouble. Yet, it would feel so good. A small payback.

"Tsk, tsk, tsk. That not be why you here," Shat'tow says.

"Oh, are we back to this again? What do you want? Let me up and I will send home whoever you want me to send home, or I will find whatever you want found. But I certainly can't do it while attached to the ground."

"Tsk, tsk, tsk, tsk, tsk, tsk, tsk." Shat'tow blew out a heavy breath at the end of his chiding. "Still don't know why you are here."

"To be annoyed? I think I'm here to be annoyed."

The sagebrush branches quivered as Shat'tow laughed again.

Feeling like I'm just being mocked again, I tighten my arm muscles as much as I can and try to pull up the stake holding the tethers. If I could just get one hand free, then…

Shat'tow's ruckus stops. "Can't have that."

His voice booms now with command that hadn't been there before and the ropes cinch down on my arms. I give one last effort, but the restraints clamp down with no give at all. I give up, relaxing my body, which is now held uncomfortably even with the sand as a cushion.

At this point, I will say just about anything to get up. "All right. Why am I here?"

"Just to be held tight." Shat'tow nods. "That's what Shat'tow was told to do. Hold you tight."

"Who told you this?"

"Shat'tow's friend." He nodded singularly and deeply with these words.

"Only have one, do you?" I mutter under my breath. However, I do feel a sad echo. Some could say that Jason is my only friend, and one that I pay. Would Jason stay around if I weren't his boss? Everyone else just comes by to see me when they need something from me. How depressing.

I shake the disparaging thoughts from my head and get back on track.

"We could be friends, my man," I say. I do not put a touch of enthralling power behind it. Firstly, I don't want snake venom dumping down my throat while I am completely unable to do anything about it. Secondly, I am interested to see if I can actually befriend him for real. Maybe I'm here because this is something we both need.

Even as I realize this thought, I sense the truth of it. Not once has the fabric of this world – which I must presume is Midgard for I've had no indication otherwise – given an anxious ripple of things going wrong. Instead, the fabric has been calm. At least when I'm here with the odd sagebrush man.

"Shat'tow is friend, by holding you down. Not see now, but you will," Shat'tow says as he points with his index finger as if he's giving a lecture.

"So, you were told to do this and you are because you're my friend?"

"Exactly!" Shat'tow wiggles as he settles back down into the sand and then he closes his eyes. "Time to move on. I try to do better this time."

What did he mean by that? Before I can ask, Shat'tow begins his meditative chant once more. I find myself sliding along the hum and disappearing.

CHAPTER 8

There is a fatal flaw, and I, of course, see it the moment that I hear the mechanical *whaaa-pauk, whaaa-pauk* even before I open my eyes to a cloudless blue sky and the dastardly sound of destruction making dust-like clouds float above me.

Nothing about this is good. I'm here at my house, alone and without Fenrir. I really doubt he's returned, not when he enjoying the cooing attention of all the women.

Evidently, my thoughts were astray as I figured I would reappear in the Amazonian hall. But no, that would be too simple.

I have manifest flat on my back on the lawn with these mechanical devices destroying my house. With Fenrir, I could get back to the Amazons. As it is, I will have to find another way. That probably means breaking a Valkyrie hair. That doesn't make me very happy, but neither does the destruction of my house and property. You'd think that after they had summoned me the first time and seeing that I would help with their missing spear, they would've called off their attack.

Of course, now that I think about it, I'm not quite sure why they would've attacked me to begin with. Why is this happening?

I am failing to grasp something. But what exactly am I missing? What is so obvious about the situation that I can't see it even though it is right literally in front of my face as clearly as I see the underbelly of one of the tank-like machines rolling over me. I have come dangerously close to landing beneath one of the spiked plates covering their tread which impale the ground and tear it to shreds as it lifts.

I am so not amused, but I'm also aware that I need to get up now. As soon as the vehicle clears me, I jump to my feet. On unsteady ground, I realize that I am back in female form as my heels shake beneath me. At this rate, I'll be lucky to last the day without breaking a shoe. Right now, I'm pretty sure they are so filthy that there will be no salvaging them without a bit of magic and possibly some illusion. It's a terrible thing to have to waste power on clothes.

"Stop it," I shout. At first, it sounds highly immature, like a bratty child. Then I see them starting to react and I get more forceful. "Stop it now!"

The voice of a mother yelling at the brat.

There's a fleeting thought at the back of my mind as I watch the chaos around me come to a standstill, and that thought is one of wondering if me remaining a woman in this scene was what the sagebrush man had meant when he said he'd try to do better this time. Could it be that he is the one controlling all of this?

Then the thought is gone as I face what is happening around me.

It feels surreal, this dust and destruction around me and the dappled sunlight trying to penetrate the clouds caused by the havoc. It's almost like it is an illusion, a strange dream that feels so real but is still just a dream. I reach out to see if there is magic here.

"You tell them, Papa!" Fenrir barks as he runs up to me.

If anything ever confirmed that this is an illusion, this was it. Fenrir would never leave the comfortable spot he has with the Amazons to come back here. This knowledge relaxes me like a warm cup of coffee between my cold hands.

But why would someone do this, and who is behind it?

"Papa, shall I take you to see who is behind all this?" Fenrir asks as if he can read my mind.

Now, it often feels as if Fenrir can read my mind, but as I know this is not my son, it's clear that that is not the case. In fact, it all feels staged, just like everything else about this horrible scene. Someone has been reading my mind and locating the exact event which what would make me very angry: having what is mine taken from me. The true joke is that here on Midgard, anything can be taken away and replaced. My anger is unjustified.

But let's face it, gods just aren't used to playing that way. We're used to having our heart's desire. It's been interesting to see humans beginning to possess that same characteristic. Might it be one of the reasons that the fabric of Midgard so willingly took me in?

I really don't have time for analysis now. But certainly interesting thoughts I will have to consider another time.

"Papa? Shall we go?" Fenrir asks insistently.

Someone knew me well enough to know that I'd want to get away from here and make this stop.

"No," I say firmly, determined to stand my ground. I wave my hand and pull off the illusion costuming Fenrir to discover it is really a goat in disguise. It bleats at me almost as if it was laughing. "Where is he?"

With another bleat, the goat turns and bounces off into the dust. I follow, pulling off all the magic from around me as I go. The brick driveway restores to the beautiful pathway that I adore. My grassy yards no longer looks ripped up. My house is no longer split in two. Trees torn asunder right themselves into the ground again. Dust settles back to the earth.

When all is righted, there is only one other person standing near me.

"Brother," Thor calls out so loudly that I flinch. He glances me over. "Or should I say, Sister?"

I can feel it coming. What always happens whenever I take a female form and Thor comes around. It's unbearable, and I wait for it as if I'm waiting for an ice cream cone to arrive.

"Can we go catch a unicorn now? Please?" Thor asks, clapping his hands together.

His fascination with horned animals is just amazing. He's the whole reason that Vikings are now pictured with horns on their helms. It truly is all his fault and has no basis in reality. Now he wants me to play along again.

"Thor," I say, trying to have patience, "how many times do I have to tell you that there are no unicorns left on this world. It's forsaken. If anyone can save Midgard now, it's me. I am your last unicorn."

His lips press tightly together and he gives me a long, level look. I see the wheels turning as he seeks a way to turn the adventure. I decide I must stop him before he goes on another tangent.

"What are you doing here," I ask, "and why are you doing this?"

I don't mention the spear at this moment. I want to see if he'll trip himself up with it first. It might be best if I pretend that I don't know anything about it.

Thor grins. "So strange that you should ask me what I'm doing here."

CHAPTER 9

I don't know what it is about those words, or maybe more specifically it is just the word "here" that is the catalyst, but I really am tired of being teleported whenever someone says something along the lines of why someone is here.

This thought locks in as I finish a solitary blink and am suddenly back in the Amazonian hall, save that it is now empty except for Becca. No, she's Gelsh now. Her hair is longer and those sunlight-filled curls cascade all the way down her back to her hips. She's dressed in a white gown with golden edging. The helm covering her head and coming down across the bridge of her nose is golden with white wings. There are fortune runes written across the forehead of her helm. In her right hand, she holds a spear upright.

Damned if she doesn't look perfect.

Her blue eyes had been cast downward toward the marble floor, but she now raises them slowly. "Laufey," she says with almost the same measured pace as lifting her gaze.

I am still in female form. I cannot tell you how much that

hurts, for me to see her like this and for her not to see me as I wish she would. I feel so much pain in that moment that it surprises me. There is nothing else for me to do but swallow my emotions and deal with the moment.

Argh!

Okay, I'm ready.

Chills sweep down my arms as I suddenly don't know what to call her in return. Is she Becca or is she Gelsh? Oh, somewhere there is a god behind this and laughing at the revenge they are having in tricking me. How dare they toy with my emotions for their own amusement?

I desperately search for something to say, something that can follow her merely speaking my name. How does one pick up a conversation like that, especially not knowing what to call someone.

"Yes?" I say.

Lame!

Surely I can come up with something better than that.

"Nice spear," I add.

Double lame!

"I know why you've returned, Laufey, and you will not take the spear from my hands."

Why do people always assume that seeing me means that I'm going to steal something? Geez!

"I see no better place for it than in your lovely hands," I say, being completely honest.

"I'm serious, Laufey. I cannot let you take this spear."

Okay, well, sheer honesty isn't working, so I might as well play along. "I don't think I want it. Doesn't look very impressive to me. Does it do anything special? Sing? Dance? Forecast the end of the world? Strike presidents with boils?"

At this point, I'm realizing that this might be a pre-timeline of some sort. Yet, it's strange. She has the spear, yet it was after the spear was stolen that I was introduced to her as Laufey. It is a realization that makes me smile. Clearly, the spear is returned to her since the introduction. That's good. Yet, she doesn't acknowledge that I was the one who returned it to her, so that's bad. The universe at large is just not letting me catch a single break on this one. Or, maybe I am in male form when I return it to her and I, as Loki, am the hero. If that's the case, I could forgive all of the universe's prior transgressions.

"Someday, you will regret all your misdeeds," she says.

Yep, I would say that my regrets started about five minutes ago.

"You can't regret the things you do not do," I say, letting my voice be level and calm. In taking my mother's name, I have a clean slate. I will not let Becca/Gelsh accuse Laufey unjustly and for things she has not done. It's one thing to blame me, Loki, for mischief, and another to blame Laufey for misconduct when by that name there has been none.

At least that I'm aware of. At this moment. What's to come in the future… well, I make no promises about that.

"You disappoint me." The Valkyrie gives a shake of her head.

Enough already! I'm done being a disappointment for something I have not committed.

Why does Becca consistently get this rise out of me? She chides me and I take offense at her every word. It's not fair to me. It's probably not fair to her either, but … she gets under my skin. Why?

"Good," I say to her. I feel sharpness in my eyes, a venom I wish I could feel in my heart, but I don't harbor anything of the sort. Still, she has hurt me and I feel the need to seek retribution for these slights. I take a bow, forgetting for the moment that women curtsey. "May I continue to delight in your disappointment."

Tears spring to her eyes. "I was hoping you'd come to apologize and that we could be friends again."

Oh, this is too much. I wish I had some clue to what had happened. First, she's sour, now she's emotional. Pick one, girl, and stick with it. I'm getting mixed signals.

I must break this poor stalemate. "Gelsh, I truly do not want the spear. It belongs in your hands. Now, if you'll excuse me, I must be going."

How I would make myself be gone without excessive magic, breaking a Valkyrie hair, or Fenrir, I don't know. But at this point, I will do nearly anything to save face. Just disappearing will be worth whatever the end cost might be. Returning to being the bookkeeper needing to get to the meeting with her boss would be a welcomed end to this situation.

I wonder if just closing my eyes for a long moment will trigger me moving on.

What is causing my leaps?

Somehow, I doubt it's blinking. It's never blinking. No, it's more likely to be someone powerful and vengeful pulling on an astral thread according to their whim. Tug, and I'm yanked to a new spot.

I pivot back toward Gelsh, my high-heeled shoe scrapping on the marble as I turn. I give a little lick of my lips as I prepare to say the burning question on my mind. "Gelsh, how did you get the spear out of the comet? When Thor plants something in a rock, it doesn't come out easily."

Gelsh shifts her weight back and forth, fingers flexing around the spear as if solidifying her hold. "I…"

Her eyes fill with the fear of not knowing what she is going to say. She doesn't know how to answer.

The fabric of Midgard ripples and an image comes to me. Gelsh had said we were friends. She calls me Laufey, but instinctively she knows I am Loki, the one who she could expect the mischief of stealing the spear, but also she said we were friends and a very long time ago, we were. If Thor had driven the spear into the comet, it would take his strength to get it out. There's scant possibility that I would be able to do it. It's really time to get back to Thor.

"Relax," I say, an uncontrollable urge taking me over. "I've got to go see the boss first, but don't worry. I know why I'm here."

CHAPTER 10

I t must be those words.

I find myself back in the dated office at the manufac-turing plant, cream colored walls, uncomfortable office chair, whirling computer, and all. It's like I never left.

"I know what I'm doing here," I say, ready to find myself with the funny sagebrush man again. Only he stands between me and Thor now.

I blink.

Same walls.

I close my eyes. "I know what I'm doing here."

Nothing.

Maybe someone else has to say it, or perhaps it involves having another person in the conversation. Spells like this, as simple as they might be to trigger, can have complex compo-nents to them, like a safeguard to make sure that when I figured it out – and I did! – that I couldn't force the magic to activate at my will.

I am tempted to fetch the secretary to be my partner in

making the next leap. Once I do, I will have Shat'tow to help me jump to Thor. Now that I've got the hang of this, it's almost like a fun carnival ride.

The computer stops at a login screen before I vacate my chair. I waste little time in deciding to type in the password. I suppose that it wouldn't hurt to have the computer finish cycling up and loading everything while I make another round of jumps. I can't trust Thor not to say something stupid and fling me back to the Amazons. Besides, this is where I started my leaps, as I was coming in to finish a case, so I must presume that there is something here for me to do as well. Meeting this boss might be important. Because it is so odd, I wonder if that boss is Thor. If I could use two of these jumps to speak with Thor, I'd have twice the number of chances to get myself out of these loops. As fun as they are, I really do have other cases I must be working on. I am far too busy to dally like this. Yet, there must be something in each of these spaces that relates for nothing is ever truly random.

The computer takes barely any time at all to come up and show me a desktop loaded with three columns of icons. One sits alone in the middle of the vacant section of the monitor. It is a document labeled, "Loki." If that isn't just the damnest thing.

I reach for the mouse, realize that it has no power, flip the underside switch to on, and go to click the icon.

Just beneath the cursor as I reach the document, the computer gives a ding and a button pops up at the same time I go to click. The computer gives no hesitation in answering the incoming calling it just received. There is no chance to back out or even straighten myself as the camera shows me on the screen along with the boss I was to have the meeting with.

It's not someone I don't know though. The surprise startles

me and I get the same reaction mirrored to back to me from the person on the other end of this meeting. It's Jason.

"Hi, boss," I say, possibly a bit too chipper. The humor of this situation is not lost on me. Again, the universe trying to make fun of me. "What's up?"

Jason, however, is completely unamused. Typical. Twice he tries to speak, his mouth forming a letter like a W as if he's going to ask what is going on or what am I doing in this meeting. As if I have any more answers than he does right now.

His lips tighten seriously and he leans forward toward the monitor.

"The plant numbers must go up," he says. His eyes get a little shifty as he finishes the sentence.

He really does look a bit nervous.

"Yeah?" I ask. The non-committal question should give him lots of leeway to say something informative.

"If we're going to get there, we must strengthen our team," Jason continues.

"You're the boss." I can't help saying it without a chuckle. "Unless you want to fire me. Good time to do it."

Jason's face holds no emotion though his brown eyes are staring right at me as if he's willing me to understand what he's thinking. I'm a god, not a mind-reader. If only he knew what I was thinking.

"Our stakeholders are most unhappy and they might spearhead a campaign for control," Jason says.

Ah. He's not alone, and I'd say that someone has a weapon held against him. A spear perhaps? A spear that the Amazons are looking for. Hmm, I wonder.

"Truly," I answer. "I am getting a little sense of that. Is it merely the plant number they want to go up?"

"I think they wish to consolidate. There's another plant

they want to go down. Once it's put out of commission, profits will point in a steady direct upward."

Jason's words are clearly calculated and measured so that he can inform me of what is happening on his end, or at least what his captors want to pass along to me. I am not sure which it is. The Golden Fleece makes Jason immortal; it would wrap around his shoulders like a boa constrictor if he were in any true danger. Since it isn't on him, either his captors are aware of the situation around Jason, or they haven't threatened him enough for the Fleece to make it's appearance. Jason does hold himself cautiously so that it only appears when he absolutely needs it. That Fleece cost him everything so he doesn't like pulling it out unless necessary.

But for me to decipher what he is trying to tell me, especially if he is in danger and not wanting the Fleece to present itself, must be taking careful restraint on his part. It's little wonder he's trying to keep his emotions out of this conversation.

Clearly, Jason is referring to a spear. Keeping such a weapon with the point down is a clear way to dull it. So, one always holds a spear upright. Hence the reference to profits in an upward direction. Got that. But a plant being shut down, what could that possibly mean? And how do they believe that I, sitting here at this desk as a bookkeeper supposedly knowing what I'm doing, close another of the company's factories. If these people really wanted something like that to happen, they should have kidnapped my bookkeeper, Betsy. She'd have more insight into doctoring the numbers than I would. Yes, I run my businesses with big decisions, but I have people to handle things like this for me so I can focus on my purpose of being here on Midgard.

"Tell me more about this plant they want closed," I say.

"It's similar to one that's close to home."

Now I don't understand his meaning at all. There are no industrial buildings anywhere near my home.

"You know I had to fly to get here, right?" I ask. Jason is the one who booked my flight, so he should know.

"Who's the boss here?" Jason says. "I'm telling you it's very close to home."

"All right. I'll get to it." Perhaps the document on the desktop labeled *Loki* has further instructions. The sooner I get out of this meeting and look at the file, the more information I hope to have.

Jason surprises me now by giving me a wink. "Good. Now, go find out why you are there."

CHAPTER 11

I am tied down in the sand once more and I completely cannot believe that Jason has betrayed me so. Did he know about the document on the computer I needed to look at? Right now, I have an overhead sun blaring right down into my eyes. I'll be lucky if I'm not blind by the time I get back to that office scene.

And what was with his wink?

I'm starting to cook in my suit. My feet are sweating and the ropes around my ankles and wrists are starting to chaff from the moisture on my skin. I turn my head, looking for the sagebrush man, Shat'tow, and I wonder if I'm back too soon and he is not prepared. He's usually squatting next to me and staring me right in the face. I feel the sandy dirt rub against my scalp.

Isn't it weird that as I turn my head, I'm not feeling my long white hair pulling? I should feel a tug as the long hair trapped under my back pulls on my scalp. Thankfully, I do feel that I do still have hair, but there's not much as if it's cut in a shorter men's style. If only I could see myself, I could tell if this were a cast illusion or not. Still, illusions don't act much more than a Halloween costume. I can't tell you how many times Thor reached out and pulled my hair even though I had a solid illusion cloaking me. He always seemed to know it was me.

Am I even in my own body right now? I dread the times I have to ask that question. It never ends well.

I pick my head up so that I can look down toward my shoes. Good ol' Oxford leather, they are. Black suit jacket is held in place by one button. White shirt beneath, which I can see as it tucks into my slacks a gap of the jacket as it falls open near the bottom hem. Still no tug on the scalp.

A trace of a memory surfaces back to me. I'd been captured, brought here, was forced to my knees, then wings – white wings – and a sword blade.

The Valkyries, they had taken me down and cut my hair. Magic for magic, they said.

I lay a quick curse – the first one I could think of -- one that could only be broken if they returned Becca to being Gelsh. It would seem they had, but they had not brought her completely back to their fold. No, they had left her with the Amazons. Close, but not quite. Certainly enough to spoil Loki's efforts and get a laugh on him.

Now I'm angry, for they had done this and tried to make me forget. No foul shred of dignity do they leave me. For all the childhood joys I remember with the Valkyrie, they now mock me as if I'm the nerd whose head they want to shove in the toilet. Against my better wishes, tears well up in my eyes. I close my stinging eyes and blame it on the sun.

Where is Shat'tow? On the one hand, I'm glad he's not

here. On the other, I could use an innocent to verbally strike out at and use words to tear him asunder.

No, it's not fair, and yes, I am feeling a little vicious. But at this rate, the universe isn't going to give me what I want anyway, so I might as well have an ounce of a temper tantrum.

Now that I have and I've taken a couple of deep breaths, I can see things so much more clearer. It all ends in one question: why would the Valkyrie want my hair?

I'm not as vain as Sif and I've done my penance for stealing her hair. So what do the Valkyries want?

Let's look at this from another angle, shall we? My hair is shorn, broken and not left a full strand. They could have plucked me bald. I do liken this attack to me breaking the Valkyrie hairs for magic as I used to have to do in the recent past and still do sometimes to cloak my actions. Yet, how does that relate to right now, and what else is going on? I must examine everything.

In these scenes I am rotating between, Jason is my boss, rather than me being his boss. So we have the broken hairs and the change in position. These things point to the one who has arranged this. I still can't see the whole picture though to know who it is.

In addition, we have a spear that is involved in a shifting timeline. And Jason's wink; that is a mystery in and of itself. He was clearly trying to communicate something.

Where is Shat'tow?

If he doesn't come, how will I be able to activate the spell and move on back to Thor. Hmm, maybe I should rethink finding the unicorn. If I tell him we're going on his special quest, he might just come with me. I like the idea. I don't know how helpful he'd be, but I could at least show him the spear and then ask him why he took it. He might just need the visual aid to help jog his oaf of a memory.

My own thoughts circle round. It's not as if Jason hasn't winked at me before. This time just felt different.

OMG, as the kids these days say. What if Jason was the illusion? Someone pretending to be him. Not as if that hasn't happened before. But no, his shock when he saw me on the screen was genuine. I got no sense of falsehood.

Granted, that could mean whoever was being the illusion of Jason was just that good.

I can't start casting doubts on everything around me now. That's a sure way to insanity and certainly not proactive to solving this situation. Yes, if anything, I am certain now that this is all one situation, not three or four as it seems. They weave together, though I don't yet know how.

"Helllooo!" Shat'tow shouts in my face. His shadow falling over me breaks the glare of the sun. "You're back. Shat'tow missed you."

Branches stick out from the tangle of his hair in all directions and dapple sunlight. His thick lips, the green paint cracked and wearing thin on his skin, gives me a grin and splits so I see his teeth. He really is joyously happy to see me. The happy little sagebrush man.

Sagebrush... plant.

Could this be the plant Jason referred to? We live near a sagebrush steppe. The plant close to home!

"Ah, Shat'tow, so good to see you too," I say while my brain is trying to calculate at a million miles an hour. Why would someone want this sagebrush man harmed? On the other hand, he does have me tied down and that is annoying, so I might have a small(ish) understanding. "Are we done with this game now? Can we be done? I'd really like to get up.

Maybe we could share a drink together. I'm parched. You must be too. What do you say? Release the ties?"

Snake venom dumps into my mouth.

For once, I must say the curse activates as it should. I was charming with the intent to deceive. I try to push it from my mouth. A couple lone drops dribble out the side of my lips and roll across my face to trickle along my high cheekbones. Now I'd give anything to be able to wipe that wet sensation away.

"Please, don't make me swallow it," I say, but the words are lost to garble behind the fluid. I'm losing. I'll choke if I don't just man up and swallow. I certainly don't want to be coughing on my back. I hate everything about this situation.

Shat'tow looks tore between concerned action and the instinct to protect himself. He knows someone is after him. He wants to help, but he knows better than to trust Loki. Oh, foul reputation.

His hand comes to my chest and his eyes grow sad. "Have you figured out why you are here?"

CHAPTER 12

The nose-tingling earthy scent of sagebrush fades to the country odors of cut crops and dairy farms.

I find myself standing back at my house on the brick driveway, feet propped on heels. I still have the sensation of liquid on my cheek and I wipe furiously at it even though there is no remnant, not even a bitter taste of it in my mouth.

This time, I'm pretty sure I didn't even blink.

Thor stands over by Fenrir's favorite tree playing with his goat. It bounces around him as he tries to grab its horns and wrestle it to the ground. They both look spectacularly happy and I hear Thor muttering something about how the goat wants to go find its one horned cousin even if nasty ol' Loki doesn't want to go. I roll my eyes.

The sun feels unyieldingly warm on my shoulders. Not quite as hot as in Shat'tow's part of the world, but that also could be attributed to short skirt versus pants and jacket. I let myself gaze toward the few high and thin clouds that are floating effortlessly in the sky, like wisps from a painter's brush.

Somewhere, beyond those beautiful clouds, a comet streaks toward the inner part of the solar system where it will fling itself around the sun and go for another loop. For some unknown reason, Thor will (or shall) impale that comet with Gelsh's spear. As much as I like to believe Thor is dim-witted, he really isn't. Don't tell him I said that. When the event occurs, if it hasn't already, he knows exactly what he is doing.

You know, at first glance it would seem as if I am intended to use the spear after stealing it from Gelsh to kill the sage-brush man and Thor takes the spear from me and imbeds it into the comet to stop me from doing just that.

Thank goodness nothing is ever that obviously simple, am I right?

If the logical progression I construe from the elements is not the answer, then what is the answer?

With a sigh, I put myself back into this case and looking for clues which will lead me out of this situation. It still might be nice to have Thor's help to figure out about the spear, so I must recruit him to come with me.

"Still want to find a unicorn?" I call out to Thor as I walk toward him.

His head whips in my direction. "How did you get over there? Loki --" His eyes narrow as he straightens his stance and puts his hands on his shoulders. "Wait a sec. Don't tell me you haven't heard a word I've been telling you."

I can feel I'm about to be punched by Thor. For those of you concerned about Thor punching a woman, let me remind you that I'm not a mortal. Thor knows I can take it no matter what I look like on the outside. Otherwise, this would be an entirely different conversation. Part of my fun has always been pushing Thor's anger and getting out of being punched or ducking very fast when I see it coming. It's what we do as brothers who are warrior gods. Don't worry about us. It's cute that you do.

"Thor, you mutter… there are words. Somewhere… in there."

His shoulders sag and he sighs out an even deeper and more exaggerated one than I had previously upon deciding to walk over here.

"You asked me what I was doing here, so I was telling you," Thor said. "How am I supposed to answer your question if you won't even listen to what I'm saying. You know, that's a character flaw you have."

I blink at him. Did the words *character flaw* just come out of his mouth? "Who have you been talking to?"

"Loki." For a moment, his eyes are filled with shame. I'm probably wrong in delighting in it, but I do anyway.

"Yes?" I ask.

He huffs another heavy breath which leaves him wilting. This isn't like him.

Oh, damn, This is another illusion. My mouth falls open and I step backward wishing to get out of the radius of something I feel rippling through the fabric of Midgard. It's a warning, but seriously too late.

I had been so willing to stop when I cleared the other illusions that I missed the final one: Thor and his goat. Behind this pretty, glossy cloak is the answer to who is behind this. All I have to do is pull away the magic.

When I do, I find out who wishes to do me ill now.

No wonder they were so insistent on asking me if I knew why I was here. It's a grudge match.

Who have I ticked off now. Can no one take a joke? Everyone is so willing to dish out the trash, but no one can take it when Loki comes around.

I bring my hand to my mouth, blow quickly into the palm, and begin to swirl ice around under my fingers. I have a feeling I'm going to need it. But I also make the decision to play along.

If I'm still in my female form, I might as well use the wiles… because if nothing else, Thor is all male. I put on a little pout. "Thor," I say, blinking my long eyelashes, "why is your unicorn so important to you? I'd love to hear you tell me."

Proof that this is not Thor is by the way he is taken aback. In fact, it's a clue that my aggressor isn't male at all. At least that narrows the field down to half of the people I've ever annoyed.

"It's their flowing manes and tails," Thor says. "So beautiful, don't you think?"

Definitely not Thor, who's more into the horns. Why else would he have picked goats to pull his chariot? It would have been rhinos if I hadn't stopped him. No one in Asgard wanted all that thundering outside their halls every time Thor came to visit. But no one ever sees the good that Loki does!

Besides, I tried to talk him into antelope, which are so much cooler and so much better to eat. But no, he thought it was a trick and picked the goats to enchant. I'll never understand what he was thinking.

But manes and tails make me think about hair. I think of Gelsh's hair all long and flowing as only a Valkyrie's can. I think about mine cut short as I lay in the desert and now recall the Valkyrie cutting it from me. And I think about my hair in this scene all dark, curly, and bouncy. Someone is envious of me whether I be male or female.

"Why, Thor," I ask coolly, deciding I now have my suspect

pool narrowed down considerably, "when did it all become about the hair?"

The illusion falls away and it's as if I watch Thor melt like sad ice cream on a sweltering day. In his place stands Sif with her hands on her hips. Oh, she is a sight to see with her long golden hair which dangles all the way down to the ground. Her dress is only a shade darker than her hair and around her waist is a dark orange cloth with an apple that hangs from it.

The goat changes to a young fawn who darts behind her skirts and peers out at me with wide, innocent eyes.

The ice I'm forming in my palm liquifies as if taking on the heat of the sun. Sif's presence is that strong.

"It's been about the hair since you took mine," Sif says. "Now, I'm going to have my revenge. When you get back here, you're not going to like it. So, why don't you go figure out what brought you to this point and why you are here."

CHAPTER 13

Thespell tugs slowly this time and I get a clear glimpse of
Sif's snarling smile as I disappear. She really intends on
reeking some havoc. I am in for it now. Whatever she has
planned, it's not good.

As I land back in the hall of the Amazons with Gelsh
holding the damned-able spear, I wonder how quickly I can
get back to Sif. But, I want to figure out what is going on with
Gelsh too.

Oh, look how the ladies have Loki torn! If ever the fabric
of Midgard or even the greater Universe at large was going to
laugh at me, it's now.

Focus, Loki.

Yes, Gelsh, spear, marble columns. Check. What am I
doing here? What is going on?

"Are you just going to stand there and stare at me,
Laufey?" Gelsh asks. "It's getting old."

"Sorry," I say reflectively. Speaking of old, I'm feeling a

little like that right now myself. Maybe I am getting too old to do this anymore. Time to give up chasing the Valkyrie!

"Well?"

Damn. I'm still staring.

"Um…" Classy, Loki. Classy. Would you damned well think of something to say? "So, how'd you get the spear?"

Lame. Was that really all I could think of saying? I really am losing my touch.

Gelsh also gives me a look which expresses just how unimpressed she is. At the moment, I'm glad she sees the female version of me and not the me she knows. As another woman, I can look goofy and she won't hold it against me.

"Really? That's the question you're going to ask now?" she asks with sharpness in her tone. "You know I'm not going to answer and give you the opportunity to step back in time and grab it before I even get there."

Okay, good point. I would do exactly that.

If I were Loki and she knew it. But she clearly doesn't. So instead I'm left with the mystery of what I have done.

An idea overtakes me. "If I put my arms behind me, would you allow me to come closer and check out your spear?"

The end of the spear loses contact with the ground as she widens her stance and braces the spear in her hands.

"On my honor," I say, quickly putting my hands behind me. "What is this world coming to when one woman doesn't believe another?"

Valkyries… long time champions of feminine power. Hit them there in their center and they crumble. I see it in action as she softens her stance and sets the spear upright once more.

"Come," she says, beckoning me with a hand that then goes to hilt of a robust dagger hanging from her belt.

I am careful not to look away from her deep blue eyes as I move forward though my gaze really wants to seek out and follow the dance of her blonde curls. Every step, I feel myself being pulled into the warm orbit that surround all Valkyries to welcome souls of the dead away from the cold chill of death.

As I draw closer, her eyes narrow. "I know you. You're not…"

She struggles to find the words and I know she's sensing Loki rather than Laufey but her mind can't comprehend it in the way it needs to in order to grasp what she is feeling. Mind and heart are at odds with what they know and see.

"Do not worry about it. It's nothing," I say, enchanting the words with charm.

She falls under the spell and relaxes. I probably could have entranced her so that I could walk right up and examine the spear outright, but that might have triggered the snake venom. I doubt I could mesmerize her enough to take the spear; that would trigger her defenses. Keeping it light and soft, practically undetectable, seems my best route.

Careful to keep my hands behind my back as I had promised – even though I really want to reach out and touch the spear — I draw closer to her. The spear is, of course, magical. It's in the hands of a Valkyrie. How could it not be magical?

Her eyes remain soft, though apprehensive. She still isn't completely trusting of me. That's okay, I wouldn't trust me either if our positions were reversed.

The spear is a beautiful lime green and silver metallic. The shaft is smooth save for a crosscut grip around the middle of the shaft and two little black bands containing etched symbols at the top and the bottom edges. The tip itself looks as if it's a

Native American arrowhead. It does look stronger than obsidian, but it might be reinforced by magic. It is an elegant mixture of historic and futuristic.

"What does it do?" I try to carefully overlay my words with the subtlest enchantment to coerce her to tell me, but I don't want to lay it on too thick. I know how easily it can backfire on me. I just want her to feel comfortable enough to answer me. I would think that would be a small enough request.

"You have seen it, now step back." Her hand slides down to the grip pad. Her fingers are so long and beautiful that one might expect to see long painted nails adoring the ends. But not the Valkyrie. They keep their nails trimmed short and clean. Hers are not quite cut down to the quick but do leave just a hint of white above the top. Nails can be an effective weapon and there is no part of a Valkyrie that they don't consider unusable.

I back up as she requested. It will do me no good to antagonize her. I am liable to get more cooperation out of her for the information I want if I work with her.

I just wish I knew what the spear had to do with all of this. If this is about Sif's revenge for me once taking her hair – OMG, that was a long time ago and I thought we'd settled it – then what is the point of this spear? Is someone else wanting me to take the spear and use it against Sif? That would explain why Thor would bury it in a comet, since Sif is (was, maybe?) Thor's wife. Matrimony among gods is a strange thing and I refuse to explain it to you mortals now.

Back to my chain of thought, and if that is the intention, then someone else has it out for Sif. That I could believe. I mean, did you see the cuteness of that fawn with its wide, innocent eyes? Not everyone can be a fertility goddess with apples and a fawn at her side. If Thor ever wanted to catch a unicorn, why does he not ask his wife?

What am I doing in the middle of all this?

It's a good question and I raise my gaze to meet Gelsh's. Before I realize what I'm saying, I ask, "What am I doing here?"

CHAPTER 14

Damn. I hadn't really meant to trigger the spell, but I did. Can't a guy (or girl) ask an honest question?

I have an odd, momentary sense of vertigo as the cream-colored walls of the office come into view and I feel myself settle into the back-aching office chair. The spell might be fading or running out of power. I'm noticing the shift more and more.

Jason still stares at me from the computer screen. I wonder if the meeting is frozen until he blinks. "Loki?"

"Shh! Don't say anything," I say, quickly reaching for the mouse. I quickly minimize the meeting window to go back to the desktop. Right there is the file labeled: *Loki.* I put the blinking mouse pointer over it, but don't click just yet. I want to make sure something isn't going to pop up like it did for the meeting with a boss who turned out to be Jason.

Nothing appears.

I double click and the file opens.

The font size in the document is really small. So tiny, in fact, that it's illegible.

"Damn," I say. "Jason, how do I increase the font size of a document?"

"What do you see?" he asks, a disembodied voice coming through the speakers. At least he managed to withhold a sigh from his voice, though I'm sure if I could see him, I'd notice him rolling his eyes. Granted, he doesn't know I minimized the video. I like to think that he is straining to not roll his eyes in fear that I'm watching him.

"I see a little document. You know, one of those type-y typed ones."

"Is the page of the document small or is the type small?"

He's pushing me. This is not the sort of thing that I handle. I have people for this.

Jason must realize from my delay that I don't know how to answer his question. "Can you share your screen with me? That way I can see what you're looking at?"

Now he really is asking a lot from me, but at least I've watched him do this many times in our meetings with other businesses, so this is something I can handle, if not deftly. Hey, in my long existence, computers have been around for the equivalent time of a blink of the eye. Don't mock me.

"Oh, you need to zoom in," he says once he views what I'm seeing. He proceeds to tell me how to do that.

Before the words become fully visible on the screen, I stop. I don't know what kind of trap I might be walking into here. Clicking on a document made by someone else but that bears your name might not be the wisest course of action. There is something here which they wish me to see, but that doesn't mean it's a friendly narrative about how this story is going to turn out. Words have power. Since I couldn't view them, I have to expect this to be a trap.

"End the meeting, Jason." I hope my tone leaves no room for argument. With as long as we've been working together, I expect he knows my overall intent to keep him safe.

I suspect that Jason does nod, but before he closes out, he says, "Call me."

It's now that I recall that wink he gave me before the spell activated last time. I wish I'd had him text me an answer about that, but the screen is blank and the meeting closed before I can say anything further. I guess he was taking me very seriously.

I stare at the still blurry words written over the full page of the digital paper and hesitate to move forward. Not for long though, mind you. You always know what I say about that.

Gods don't feel fear.

Yep. But, that doesn't mean we can't be cautious. And cautious I am. To pull off the stunts and shenanigans that I do takes a strategic thinking mindset. Yes, even gods have mindsets. I like to know what I'm getting into and I have a good sense for how things will work out.

That little self-reminder secures my confidence. I'm ready for whatever will come. Let's do this.

I zoom in on the document.

The words remain stationary on the page. There's no firestorm of activity that whips up around me. I am not suddenly transformed back to the male version of me with my long white hair and wool cloak with the runes from Frigga down the front. Nothing changes.

In near shock and ample curiosity, I lean forward to read the document now and actually articulate what it says:

> *Loki was one of the Norse gods. No one liked him because he was a bully and picked on the other gods. The only way the other gods could get back at him was by calling him a Trickster. That way, everyone knew that he was the one who played jokes on everyone.*
>
> *They also told many stories about him, like when he stole Sif's hair. No one wanted anyone to not know about Loki and what nasty tricks he played on people.*

The document continues on like that for a while, but I read no further. It's a child's school paper… written about me! I could nearly be over the moon with joy. You think I jest, that I'm playing tricks with you too, but this kid understands. Okay, *bully* is a bit over-the-top, but for the most part the kid got it right. Might as well have added that no one liked me around and that I heralded trouble. It's not like many of the gods have come to visit me since I got kicked out of Asgard. That hasn't changed now that I'm tied to Midgard either.

So, this is most likely a document the last person to sit at this desk used to print out the page for a child (I imagine a son) to hand in for homework at school. That person kept it small so that the boss wouldn't see it while it was open to print. She probably didn't even put a quarter into petty cash to pay for her print-out. And they call me nasty.

Jason will get a laugh out of this one. Me, worried about a kid's school paper. I close down the document and reach for my cell phone. Jason wanted his call.

My eye catches movement behind me and I swivel on the uncomfortable office chair. An attacker lunges at me, spear raised over his shoulder. It is so like the green one that Gelsh had been holding, but this one is a light blue metallic rather than green. I arch my back to dodge the weapon as it comes down. This thrusts me back in the chair.

The arrowhead tip sheers across the desk and cuts a long groove into the surface. Boss isn't going to be happy about that.

Momentum carries the attacker a couple steps forward. I only get the sense that this person is not from Midgard as I reach instinctively out.

My hand comes into contact. "Skreli farhausten kjord."

Typically, everything goes with the transdimensional I return to their home realm, but in this case, the spear drops and clatters to the floor.

As I pick it up, I understand why: it belongs to another home realm, one much closer than the attacker I just sent back.

It's with a strange sense of accomplishment that I feel ready to leave. I hold the spear with the tip upright. "I know why I'm here."

CHAPTER 15

The weakening spell drags me along, the light blue metallic spear still in my hand. I'm glad that it gets to come with me.

I'm not ready for what happens next.

I appear, female me, in the sandy desert. My heels sink into the sand and I immediately have to kick them off. Now I stand in my nylons in the sand. But flat-footed in this case is so much better.

There's a lot of sagebrush and rabbit brush around me. Except for the sand, it does remind me of the desert around the canyon near where I live. There's prickly bits of thorny branches scattered in the sand around me. I'm really thankful that I didn't step on one.

The male version of me remains tied down in the sand nearby. That means Shat'tow must be close, but where? He could easily be curled over to look like a clump of sagebrush, though I'm pretty sure I'd still recognize him in camouflage from the other plants truly growing from the desert. Even in this case, a human could distinguish a costume from the real thing.

Yes, I woefully see that my hair has been cut.

Short-haired Loki has his eyes closed against the harsh sun overhead, so he doesn't yet know I'm standing there. Won't he be in for a surprise?

I thrust the base of the shaft into the sand, sticking it in probably as deeply if not more than my shoes, so that the spear stands upright.

Knowing the crazy sagebrush man might appear to stop me, I hurry to the first stake tethering male me's arm to the ground and yank it from the sand. Loki must feel the sudden slack on the line because as I near his foot, I hear him call out, "What is going on?"

"Hi. Just you saving you," I say as I pull the second stake and start for the next one holding the other foot.

"I would say so." Loki lifts his shoulders up and rolls so that he can reached the last remaining stake holding down his other arm. "Tell me… how bad is the hair?"

I stop to really take a look at the other version of myself. I know that I'd want the truth. "They clearly didn't take it from you easily. You're going to need a good barber, and you'll probably end up looking like Jason for a while." I'm seeing it in my head and it makes me laugh. "Spend some time out in the sun and everyone may think you are his gorgeous blond brother."

He sneers at this, but inside I suspect his wheels are turning too. He knows that it's a delightful idea that would so annoy Jason for a good long while. Maybe even long enough for my hair to lengthen out halfway down my back. How long could I pull off such a fantastic charade?

Loki is shedding the bonds around his ankles now that he's gotten them off his wrists. I help him to his feet.

"Nice spear," he says, his tone a touch sarcastic as he glances over the weapon.

This is when I realize that I'm really not ready for being here. "How are there two of us?" I ask. "How long have you been here?"

"I'd say a while," Loki says. "Not sure though. The memories of how I got here are coming back slowly. How long have I been female on Midgard? You didn't mess up anything for me, did you?"

"Do you still think that my illusions are that weak? Don't worry. Everyone saw me exactly as they needed to." I'm not going to let me pick on myself. Negative self-talk is never cool, especially when it's two actual versions of yourself doing it. I imagine this is what twins feel like. "I have been a woman for longer than I am used to though. I think it's worried Jason a bit too. I suspect he's been doing research on the times I've been female because I've had a few odd questions from him."

"That must be hysterical."

"Always." And we both laugh. Loki gets it.

"But now," I ask, "what are we going to do about this. Being a male is certainly less expensive than being a gorgeous female."

His mouth drops open and an aghast huff comes out. "Please tell me you haven't blown a fortune for a new wardrobe?"

"No, you've done a good job keeping me stocked, but mani's and pedi's sure have gone up since the last time."

"Ah, woman!" he growls, but I know I'm just mocking myself. As we finish another laugh together, he looks at me seriously. "So we've been separated for a while then? How long?"

"A couple months."

"Clearly you couldn't change back?"

"No. I tried a couple of times. All I could do was cast an illusion over myself at best."

Loki nods. "They must have had some spell over me. Made me all forgetful and woozy."

I know he's referring to the Valkyrie. "I agree. It felt that way when I first came here as you."

"This is getting weird," he says. He suddenly looks lost and forlorn. "They're Valkyrie, the ones who did this."

"I know. It's not a reason to forgive them though." Man, if he is like this now, wait until he learns that Becca is once again Gelsh. I'm just not sure this other version of myself can handle that right now, but we have to do something.

It's very odd when part of yourself doesn't know something. Could this be how people with split personalities feel? Interesting. I do wonder if this is something I can replicate on someone else just because it would be fun to watch someone else suffer through this. Jason perhaps? It might lead me to figure out how that Golden Fleece knows when to go to him. Certainly sounds like a good laugh or two, don't you think?

Alas, we must be moving on.

I wonder where the sagebrush man is. The fact he hasn't shown up yet sticks in me the wrong way.

"Any idea where Shat'tow went?" I ask Loki.

"He's usually around annoying me from nearby. I don't think he goes far away."

"Tell me something I don't know."

"Um, Loki?" he says, and I turn at his odd tone.

Shat'tow crouches on the other side of Loki. Half hunched

over as if his knees don't want to straighten so he can stand erect, he looks as if the sagebrush branches coming out of him want to weigh him down. I realize they are not a costume; these branches really are growing out of him. I can see where the skin at his neck raises up the same way dirt around a tree trunk does around where the branches come out of him. He holds a metallic white spear in his hands and the tip is pressed against Loki's ribs.

So much for the cheerful sagebrush man.

"He stays," Shat'tow says, nearly a shout. "He is here because he must stay."

"Give me that," Loki says as he deftly twists the spear from Shat'tow's hand. "One does not send a plant to take on a warrior."

The plant has been shut down, I realize with startling clarity as the sagebrush man shrinks back from an attack he is afraid will be next. But Shat'tow is right. Loki must stay.

I reach over and take the spear from Loki while his grip is relaxed. "Sorry, this isn't about you," I say. "You do have to stay here for a bit. I know why I'm here."

Two spears in hand, I feel pulled toward Gelsh.

CHAPTER 16

Arriving on scene with a spear in hand was a good idea. Arriving with a spear in each hand, not so much.

I'd forgotten how quickly I needed to get back to Sif, how angry she was, and that I knew I was in trouble. Damn my distractions!

Now that I'm back and once again looking Sif in the eyes, I realize I should have keep rushing through the loop. She is ang-gry! Maybe that should all be capitalized: ANGRY! I'm not sure that one exclamation point does it justice.

I'd almost think that she means to do me physical harm, except… well, gods. That's easier said than done.

So I stand there, matching her stare for glare. I won't move unless she does first. I do ready illusions of myself. I'm calm, not stupid. Confident, and only a little brazen.

I still don't know what all she's done and she's had some time to set traps while I dallied with clearing her illusions she'd created. But she does forget that she stands on my land. This is my hall, and though it is in Midgard, it is all mine.

"You're a criminal, Loki," Sif shouts at me finally.

"Correction: I'm a trickster. Having a sense of humor does not make one a villain."

Her eyes burn with the fire of her irritation and I suspect she wants to slap me. I'm surprised that she doesn't. Is she afraid of Thor's wrath? Him punching me is one thing, but he might not like another striking me. You know, it's his game that he plays with me and no one else is allowed.

I'm clearly getting nowhere with her. Time for a different tactic. "All right, Sif. Please tell me why I'm a criminal now?"

"You killed little Sava's sister."

Sava? I quickly wonder, but then I see Sif vaguely pointing toward the fawn at her side.

"Go, Sava. Take your revenge," Sif says.

The fawn looks up at Sif with wide eyes, then steps hesitantly toward me. Sava leans forward to sniff me and glances back at Sif before going to lick my hand.

"What? You're not the one?" Sif stamps her foot as she stares at me demanding an answer. "How can you not be the one?"

"Look, Sif, I don't exactly travel back to Asgard a whole lot these days if you haven't noticed. I certainly wouldn't come to kill your little deer."

"But Frey said it looked like she was killed by a spear and you're holding two. How could it not be you?"

"Did Frey say that I did it?" I decide that's a wise question to ask. There is time that my masculine self doesn't remember. Who's to say what he didn't kill the deer before the Valkyrie caught up with him and sliced his hair off.

"No," she answers. That lets me breathe a sigh of relief. I would have been sunk if the answer had been affirmative. She continues, "Just the spear."

"Fair enough then." I might be able to talk my way out of this yet while soothing her anger. If I can get her to think I'm on her side for finding this wrongdoer, then at least I won't have to figure this out all by myself. Still, it chaffs to think that once again I've been painted as the troublemaker and accused without proof. I can't tell you how annoying this gets. "Did Frey say anything else?"

"No, but he left awfully quickly after that. Right after he brought the fawn back to life."

"Wait," I say, certain that I had misheard. "Sava's sister fawn is not dead any longer?"

Sif's eyes widen as if this was a thought she should have had earlier. "No. Frey restored its life, but he took her with him when he rushed out."

Now why would Frey do that. Frey had to know something and it was something that he didn't want Sif to discover. This just got curiouser and curiouser the longer it went. Without speaking to Frey, how could I know what happened? There had to be a clue.

"While I know you have no reason to believe me, my dear sister-in-law, I swear upon Thor's life that I didn't do this."

To my surprise, and even while her lips remained pursed and her eyes sad, she nods. "I believe you. Find whoever did this."

I return her convictions with my own nods. "I can do that."

After all, that was why I was here. I didn't say it, but I am certainly thinking it, and hoping that the spell is so weak that it won't trigger, or that my thoughts won't activate it either.

I remain where I'm at, though I have to wonder at the sense of it. Sif has calmed herself, but that doesn't mean she likes me by any stretch. She sure doesn't trust me. Can't say I blame her given our past. But, in my defense, she shouldn't have been hanging around with Thor if she didn't want teased too. It's what my brother and I do. Anyone entering that circle is bound to take collateral damage. She was fair game. Naturally, she always disagreed with that assessment.

Her silver eyes widen as she stares at me expectantly. "You're still here."

I grin. "I guess I am."

She flutters a hand toward me. "Shouldn't you be off? Do what you do, and all that?"

"No," I say to her smartly. I admit that I am suddenly so very proud of myself. Loki, the trickster, the genius. I'm brilliant and no one really appreciates it. Especially Sif as she looks at me with her large eyes.

"Darling," I say, knowing that I can probably only get away with it because I'm in feminine form, "Sava and her sister can't take a card. We don't know where Frey is at and we can't assume he'll pop in for a second time to save either of them if someone comes to harm them. Are you willing to take a card for them in their stead?"

Now she eyes me wearily wondering if I'm up to some trick. I can't say that I don't have ulterior motives in mind, but I am very right. The fawns would be better protected with one of my totems.

Pulling out my phone, a device which Sif glares at and takes a step away from, I open up the back and remove one of my cards. I go to hand it to her as I pocket the phone away.

She makes no move to take it. Not even the slightest lift of her hand.

Breathe, Loki. You can do this without triggering the snake venom. Everything you're going to say to her is true.

All-Father, I know I'm going to be choking and spitting in one moment. I can feel it coming.

"There's magic on the card," she says before I get myself together enough to speak.

"Of course there's magic. I can't extend my unique protections without it. But you do need to take the card. I can't force you. It has to be of your own free will."

"It's just protections?"

"Just protections."

She ends her hesitations with another nod. "All right. For the fawns."

"For the fawns," I repeat as she takes the card.

It disappears the moment she touches it and her eyes come up sharply to mine.

"Relax, it's supposed to do that. Inside my house, protected inside one of my ice jars, is a totem which will help to secure your fawns." I raise my hand toward my house. Maybe if I let her know that the thing that's protecting the deer is inside, she won't pull out any revenge on my property.

"If you pull any tricks, Loki—"

"Yeah, yeah, I know. You'll pull my entrails out my nose," I finish for her. If I had a dime for every time I heard threats, I'd have more money than I do from people's crazy needs for their cell phones.

"This isn't a time for your jokes."

I consider winking at her, but that's just not my style right now. Instead, I reach out and touch her arm. "Your fawns will be safe. I promise you. After all, this is what I do. It's the reason I'm here."

CHAPTER 17

Once again, I am back and alone with Gelsh in the Amazonian hall. Or it appears that we're alone. I don't know why I didn't notice it before, but I get the scent of more people here than meets the eye. Honestly, it makes me a little sad.

I should be irritated.

Instead, there's a depressing sinking through me, that upset sensation that one gets when they've been betrayed by someone.

If I'm going to figure out why, I must compartmentalize the feeling and put it aside. Later, I can analyze why it affected me so deeply.

As if my god brain needs that much time: *because you have feelings for her and you thought she was back among the Valkyrie you so adore because you're a git!* it tells me.

"You sigh," Gelsh says to me.

"I do." It's a hard response for me to make and I look at her with the sadness I feel shining back at her in my eyes. If only I didn't have to do this to her. But she's not really there, no matter how much I want her to be.

No matter what, even if she's not real, I don't want her to know how I'm about to betray her. I had said I wouldn't take the spear from her, but now I have to. I always had to.

I raise my hand and pull the illusion from the room.

Gelsh disappears and a dark-skinned Amazon holds the spear. Her eyes are bright as she smiles. It is their leader, Rhetallia. "I still can't let you have it, Laufey."

"I'm afraid you have no choice." I shift the two spears so that I can grip them in both hands. "I know this won't help, but I am in complete agreement that this is your spear. If you'd just give it to me and let me finish what I need to do, I can have this back to you and good as new in a flash."

"I can't do that because we've been asked to hold you in this form."

She means me as a female. I can understand why. As a woman, I am more nurturing and compassionate compared to my masculine self. I am less likely to cause trouble.

Or so they think.

At the end of the day, male or female, I am still me.

"Let's play." As I speak the words, I cast off several illusions of myself, all holding two spears. I move one step, two steps to the right as I circle my illusions up around Rhetallia. There is no possible way that she can know that I'm at her left side now.

I watch her eyes widen as she feels the initial panic. She tries to cover for it, but I have seen her worry. Some reactions are too instinctual to hide. Sorry, but suddenly facing several opponents who all look the same typically instigates one of those emotions in everyone.

Oh yeah, I'm much less likely to cause trouble as a woman. Ha ha!

Watch me.

With the two spears gripped together, I take them and ram them into her arm. She doesn't tip off balance as I'd hoped, but now comes after me. Clearly she hadn't expected me to remain in front of her.

But, I'm no longer there where I was. Now I'm on the other side of her, having traded places with one of my illusions. What a silly mortal, even an Amazon, thinking she can take on a god.

Rhetallia comes back for the fight though, obviously thinking that she can take me on. To my surprise, she lands a blow. It's almost as hard as one that Thor would have stuck. It sends me reeling out of the ring.

She chases me, stalking me down like a lioness protecting her cub. I feel the spear tip against my chest, but it reflects off as I bat the shaft away with my spears.

Why must mortals do this?

I let her take a few more swings and parry her blows. I've got to let her feel that she's doing okay at the very least. Mortals, after all, do have to try to defy gods. It's in their very nature. Once again, the people of Midgard are so very cute.

When I tire of taking my occasional hit just to make her think she isn't completely losing – again, I have to make her feel as if all her skills and training are paying off – I blow some icy breath at her cold enough to shock her system and slow her down. The moment she's gone from the initiative attack to instinctual self-preservation, I seize the spear and twist it from her hands.

"Thank you for some sparing, Leader Rhetallia," I say before she can drop to her knees in some supplicant position and ask me to put her out of her embarrassed misery as mortals always do when they lose at the hands of a clearly overpowered opponent. Don't get me started. "Next time, I'd appreciate not having to do this in heels though. Now, I'd really like the help of you and your other ladies so that we can get the fourth part of the spear, and I can put it back together again and return it to you whole."

At first, her dark eyes are set with harsh anger at having lost. When the sincerity of what I'm telling her breaks through, those lovely espresso eyes soften and she nods. "We shall help."

"Before that, I must know," I say, knowing that I must ask an important question and feeling my heart sink at what I already know will be the answer. "The Valkyrie who you were helping, she was never here and never real, was she?"

"She is," Rhetallia says. "She is here and you did speak to her."

I feel myself perk up again. That really had happened and the Amazons were aiding her. It was all I needed to know.

Inspiration strikes me like never before and I think the wide, delighted grin I give to Rhetallia even scares her a bit. She does remember who she's playing with.

"Go, gather your ladies," I say to her.

She pivots swiftly on her feet and heads away from me. I wait as patiently as I can. There is a part of me that wishes to follow and to find Gelsh. I'd really like to see for myself that she is all right, but I will take Rhetallia's word for it. Gelsh might wonder why I am coming to check up on her and I don't wish to make her suspicious. It is best that me as Laufey has no connection to her.

Minutes later, and nearly at the end of my length of patience, the Amazons return to their training hall. Each of the women has a weapon in her hands and a few have an extra strapped to their backs, arms, waists, or legs. They all ready make a formidable sight.

"All right," I say to the group. Gelsh is, of course, not with them. There's a part of me that wishes she were so I could use her for inspiration. Still, it is probably for the best as my feelings might come through and shade my task at hand. "I am about to call my brother, Thor, here. As lovely as you woman all are, your mortal-ness will never escape his notice. I must cloak you all in an illusion of sight and sound. Be strong, ladies. Remember that no matter what you see or hear, you are still Amazons."

As one, they shift to a balanced stance and issue a guttural battle-ready exclamation.

Magic extends from me in serpentine swirls as it feeds among the Amazons. At first, it looks like fog, then billows to full-grown clouds until I can see none of their number. The magic seeps away and the mist begins to fade, leaving only my illusion behind and suddenly I am standing in a ring of Valkyrie. Some are fair-skinned and others retain their native looks, but all are blond and feathered, every one of them beautiful. Or at least beautiful to me. I have so loved the Valkyrie for eons. Even as the caster of this magic and where my mind knows it's not true, I cannot help my response to their gentle softness. Not only do they look like Valkyrie, but they feel as the Valkyrie do. Every bit of what I have ever loved about the Valkyrie has gone into my enchantment.

But now comes the real test: to see if they can fool Thor.

"My sisters," I say, raising the three spears in one hand over my head. "Now is the time. I call out for my brother, Thor, to show himself."

I bring down the spears and bang the rounded ends against the ground.

Thunder rolls in the distance, starting as a faint hum, and races closer until the air around us vibrates with the sound of it all. I hear it coming down from the distant mountains, rain following in its wake. The hall of the Amazons begins to tremble around us.

With a final crack, Thor appears. He wears laced brown trousers which are a bit baggy in the thighs and tightened around his calves, and a steel blue tunic. His hands are braced like claws before him, his lips snarling back to reveal his rather large teeth. He'd come in for the attack. The burning smell of ozone flits around him. Hawkish blue eyes take in his surroundings, scanning me up and down as he comes to me, then finishing to take in the ring of Valkyrie around him.

The fight falls off his face and suddenly he looks as if he is about to cry. I find myself stunned at the turn in his reaction. He's gone instantly from one extreme to another and I cannot fathom why.

Thor drops to his knees and lets his head hang down. "I'm sorry. I did it. I killed the fawn!"

CHAPTER 18

No one is more stunned by Thor's admission than me. That's only because no one knows him the way I do. He never likes to admit his wrong-doings. Nothing ever sticks to him. He's like that squeaky clean kid who's always teacher's pet. Except he's Odin's son, so that makes it even more cosmically taunting. Worse, he's once again trying to make me the scape goat. I realize this as I clench the spears tighter in my grip.

"Thor," I say, trying my best to imitate the way the Frigga would say it, "what has happened?"

He looks up at me with watery blue eyes. "I was hungry. Venison sounded good. They aren't much bigger than my goats, so I figured anything that small would pop back to life like the goats do."

This is why my brother tries me so. How can so much inescapably flawed logic exist within one person?

I rub my hand across my face, exhale a deep and heavy sigh, then say, "Get up, you oaf."

"Not until you call Sif here." He drops his hands to his thighs and stares back at me defiantly.

Here it comes, his plan to come out of this situation as the golden boy while he paints me as the aggressor. Fortunately for me, I am ahead of his game this time. "Sif already knows that I am not the one who caused the death of Sava's sister, and she has commanded me to lead the Valkyrie in finding the one responsible. And who do we find right off but you, confessing even."

"I will apologize her," Thor says. "I tried already, but she isn't coming when I call her."

"I can't imagine why, Thor. Disrespectable is what you've been."

"I know."

I'm really getting suspicious right about now. It isn't like my brother to admit to being in the wrong. He delights in his foul behavior.

There is the fourth part of the spear.

"Thor –"

He looks back to me quickly from where his gaze had wandered to the illusions of the Valkyrie around him. I know he is mentally testing them to see if they are real or just something Loki conjured up to frighten him. I really am glad to have the spirits of the Amazons backing the spell. Thor would be a right cur if they weren't there. As it is, he curbs his usual bratty behavior.

"The spear, Thor," I say without waiting for him.

"Yes?"

"I happen to know that you put it in a comet. Why would you do that?"

Now it is Thor's turn to sigh as he gets up. He brushes off the front of his breeches at the calves where he'd been kneeling, and then stands to his full height, putting him several inches above me. "I suppose I should show you, brother. Come with me."

His large hand clasps the back of my neck. It's as if he's forgotten I'm a woman. I guess to him it really doesn't matter. He sees me as nothing other than his family. Oh, Thor.

A moment later, I'm glad that he's got a tight grip on me.

We're in space, dang cold even for me, and the ground wiggles beneath our feet which I can not see due to a swirl of gases and subtle atmosphere. Tiny particles floating in space strike at us as if wondering why we're here and wishing us gone.

Thor steadies me, helping me adjust to the slow rotation of the comet as it flies through space. As gods, we can exist anywhere, but that doesn't mean it's always comfortable. And if I'm feeling a touch prickly in tolerating this frigid and non-existent environment, I know that Thor has to be miserable.

"Do you know why you're here?" he shouts at me. For a mere human, talking in space without a spacesuit would be impossible. For us, it's difficult but not impossible, and it comes out with an abundance of lower vibrations. It makes speaking on a planet seem like we are always using our indoor voices.

My initial fear is that I'm going to teleport to the next scene. The very last thing I want to do is leave and warm up, only to be cast back here in another cycle. When that doesn't happen, I stare back at Thor. "No! I don't know why I'm here."

Thor takes me a bit more gently by the shoulders and makes me turn. The particles coming off the comet pelt against my face now, making me realize how much Thor had been shielding me until now. As he rounds me about, he points off in the distance.

Let's just say, space is very large. I don't understand why Thor is pointing because at first it looks like nothing but the emptiness of space. Oh yes, from a human's earthly perspective, the sky is filled with pinpoints of light. In a three dimensional reality, two stars in what appears to be same brightness and in close proximity in a flat constellation could in reality be billions of light years apart. Much of space has nothing. Standing on this comet, I am at the heart of a black abyss. If I look hard, I can see pinpoints of light, but there is no atmosphere to catch it so the space around me isn't like being in the center of a globe.

Thor continues to point, waiting for me to see what he is trying to show me. I stare down his thick finger, wondering if it is in the way and covering what I am to be noticing. Then I see the speck.

The sun at the heart of the Earth's solar system. As I focus my eyes, I can even see a couple black specks crossing in front of the surface, indicating planets between where Thor and I stand and that sun which blazes its life-giving rays. This comet heads right for it.

The humans in this isolated little pocket of Midgard are in clear danger. It's as if I can see the trajectory of this icy rock right toward Earth.

Thor steps back from me. The feeling that I am left with is that I am the protector for Midgard, so I must do something about this situation. I stare at the spear implanted into the comet and realize that Thor made his attempt.

It's then that I realize what he tried to do.

I turn toward him. "A lightning rod?"

Thor shrugs, but reddens with embarrassment.

"You thought you'd just call down some lightning and blow it to pieces, didn't you?" I ask, unable to keep myself from rubbing this moment in. No wonder he was really hiding. He didn't want anyone to know about his failure. Oh, Thor.

"No atmosphere," he mutters. Of course, it's with his outdoor voice, and for the same reason that he couldn't call lightning down.

I bite back my retort. With the way everything – my hair, Thor's hair, my skirt, Mjolnir – is floating, he couldn't figure that out. I shake my head at my brother.

"Was this sent by someone?" I ask. I don't even know if Thor has an answer for my question or not, but I have to see if he has any information at all. With his presence in Asgard and being able to freely (and frequently, but don't tell Sif) move between realms, there's a good chance he's heard something. Or even being in Odin's hall, he might have been privy to a conversation. Somehow he had to know that this comet was coming. He'd been out here trying to stop it before I'd even felt the comet's presence through the fabric of Midgard.

Unless someone was shielding me.

If someone didn't want me to feel it coming, then there was a good chance the comet was set on its path on purpose. It's only coincidence until that moment that it isn't.

Thor hasn't even had a chance to answer me, but my mind is racing along looking for a reason. If someone had initiated this comet's flight, it might have been done long ago. It might also have been placed within the solar system recently and given a good push, just enough to make it seem like it had gone a long way. The comet has some spin to it, so I'd be prone to think the latter the case. So, most likely done on purpose. A comet like this striking Earth could destroy the planet. That would remove the humans from this section of Midgard, but it wouldn't ultimately harm me. Yet, whoever initiated this would have to stop me from picking up on the impending danger.

Or, maybe, the fabric knew I'd be out here to save the day and never worried about it.

It boggles the mind to think about.

"I don't think they like the earthlings very much," Thor says.

"Who doesn't like them?" I fully expect Thor to say the grey aliens. That's pretty much a given and why the two have been kept apart as much as possible. If only the two races would quit looking for each other all the time! But there is another possibility to Thor's statement, one that I dread.

Of course, he has to say it.

"The other humans of Midgard."

CHAPTER 19

If Thor hadn't been visibly shivering as the cold of space needled through to his bones, I might have hit him. As it was, I edged toward mercy for him. We had to solve this and fast. Even a god, I wasn't sure how much of standing on a comet in the black cold of space he could take. Were we closer to a sun, he might have had more time.

By this time, we're attuned to the low gravitational field of the slowly rotating comet. It feels like we are still in the same spot and that we haven't moved, but I know we have. I'm fairly certain that we are now upside-down to the way we had landed. This comet is several miles in diameter and its hard to see the surface we're standing on due to the swirling, icy atmosphere. I can sense the ice it has gathered on its travels and now sheds like a snake does to its skin. A long tail has formed out behind it as if it were a proud galactic peacock.

Could it be intergalactic even?

Here's the thing about Midgard: it encompasses this whole universe. It is a whole realm including lots of space, not merely just a planet. Now, I admit that Earth is the most interesting planet in this solar system and possibly even in the Milky Way galaxy. It's why I often use Earth and Midgard as one in the same. But it is not the only planet with humans or even the only one with life. To think that would be absurd. No realm is that unimaginative in the ways that life can thrive; complex life swells everywhere. Earth of Midgard just happens to be a very fortunate one. I often think that Odin made a little menagerie here because he could. Collecting bits and pieces together from everywhere to put in one place sounds exactly like the sort of thing he'd do.

In fact, Earth of Midgard is so diverse that it makes the other planets where humans and humanoids are elsewhere in the universe seem down-right bland. If only they knew the treasures they had.

But I digress and it's cold. And boring. This is why very few races (and honestly only the most boring of them) have developed space travel. I imagine humans will enjoy space travel at first until they realize just how long it takes to get to anywhere and they will just give it up because space is so insipidly vast. Then maybe they'll be able to turn their attentions to getting along and cleaning up the issues they've caused on the world.

Again, I digress.

Honestly, if life ceases on Midgard, then I'm sure I'll go home to Asgard. Life, not boring there.

For the moment though, this poses a problem. I'm sure Thor wouldn't be here if the calculations hadn't been done precisely to strike Earth. But how he knew it was here is another question.

"Thor," I ask, my voice booming, "how did you know

about this? Did you take the fawn to have for dinner with someone?"

He looks down at his foot as he drags it through the fog. "You always think so lowly of me."

"Thor!"

"Yes. Yes, I did. Okay?"

"No, Thor." I won't let him off the hook so easily, not when my name is the one being associated with the wrong doing. "Who did you go to have dinner with?"

Thor casts his gaze away.

"Thor!"

"The transdimensional you were heading to the factory to send home!"

"Why were you getting involved in one of my active cases?" Another pertinent question would be why Bronwyn didn't tell me, but it's not like Thor announces everything he's going to do. She truly might not have known. Sif clearly hadn't known, even though there may have been references and insinuations made which pointed to me or my case which made her think I was involved; that made sense. I also must wonder if Frey knew since he took the fawn and brought it back to life. That seems to be the final piece I need in order to see the whole picture on this puzzle.

"Can you please deal with the comet, and I'll tell you everything once we're somewhere warm?" he begs.

It truly is begging. I kind of like this. It's not often I can get Thor in this position. I kind of like it.

But this is also an environment to my advantage. I can handle this cold far longer than he can. He must be starting to ache at the very least. Thor stone cold, what a sight to behold. Oh, clever Loki. That ought to be on a cup, or maybe even a sticker.

"All right, brother," I say. "Be ready to get us off this chunk of ice."

He lays his big hand on my shoulder. I can feel how cold he is becoming just by his very touch and how easily it penetrates my thin, femininely cut jacket. I put my hands on the spear and send through it not more iciness which would only make this comet harder and thicker, but the manipulative power I use to create my ice. It truly is a feat of strength on my part to resist the cold I so long to let sing over my magic.

I sense the core and wrap around it like a hand grasping onto a still beating heart. It throbs back against my magic, faint at first, then stirring. It rouses. Quickens. At once, I realize that this comet which comes into my little galactic neighborhood of the Milky Way is trying to make a journey to me. Ice coming to ice. It needs me.

And yet, my brother, Thor, would have me murder it.

I can free it if I'm clever. But what will that take? Will such an act involve shoving Thor off the comet? That won't be enough. I'd have to touch him in order to freeze him because… well, space and no gravity… and he'd feel it the moment my touch turned cold. He'd be out of here and might not take me with him. Leaving me to get back under my own power. Only a slight threat there, but Thor would be warned and he'd be waiting. We'd probably come to blows, and that's never my first option because I always come up on the losing end of that one.

There is the possibility that Thor isn't even aware of what is in this comet. I keep saying he's not the brightest and no one ever quite believes me, but please recall how he thought the fawn would pop back to life after he ate it just because it was the size as one of his magical goats, which does return to life again and again after he feasts on their bones.

On the far other extreme, I don't know the motivations of whatever lies at the center of this icy core. Thor said it was sent by "other humans." It could be a message to ask for help, or it could be something far more sinister. I have no way of knowing until I break it out.

The core shivers. The cold of space reaches it too. It feels the chilly pull of my energy and longs to come out, but knows it's dangerous out here. Space can harm it.

"Loki?" Thor asks.

My hesitation has drawn on too long. I must get to work and decide if I'm going to claim this strange interstellar being sent from the *other humans* or not. Choose, Loki, choose.

I put my other hand on the spear and lean into it a little. Now, I let the cold reach in. The comet protects the heart at the core and I can sense nothing further of its intent beyond that I am the one it wishes to reach. I must take a chance in the very same way that Odin had to take a risk when he rushed me, a runt of a frost giant baby, away from Jotunheim.

With utmost care, I let the cold in my magic seep down into the cracks of the comet.

"You're doing it, Loki," Thor cheers as the ice begins to crackle beneath our feet. Would he be so triumphant if he knew what I was really doing?

I let the magic work its way, slowly cracking apart the comet in weak areas until it has formed a disjointed egg around the heart core. I must protect the center from breaking. Much as I would form one of my ice cylinders, I pull in more ice from the comet itself, concentrating it down to the protective shell I've created. I press it in around the heart as close as I can come until I feel it tremble at my enchanted touch. We both know it will be safe in there, pillowed by my frigid magic.

The rest of the comet can be doomed.

I withdraw the cold tones and as I hear the comet begin-ning to moan from pressure, I thrust the spear's tip down into the icy egg I've created.

"Now, Thor," I say, my voice rumbling in the depths of space like a solar wind.

In the next instant we are back on the Earth side of Midgard. I am home, and I am happy. Or, at least, mostly happy.

CHAPTER 20

Now, when I say that I am home, I really mean that I am back on Earth of Midgard. As I've previously stated, it's the only planet in Midgard that really matters because everyone else is so vapid. Truly. There's a reason why transdimensionals, when they come to Midgard, choose to actually come to Earth rather than anywhere else. They all hope they can blend in with the diversity of it all. If they behave themselves, they are generally correct. You never see me going after the average Joe creature just trying to make a living. No, it's when they decide to pop their heads up and see what they can get away with that they become the tall poppy that I notice.

But I'd be happy if I weren't in the windowless office of the factory where I'd come to send a certain transdimensional being home. At least this time, Thor is with me, and he stares around at the cream-colored walls and old metal filing cabinets with a delightful look of distaste tugging his lips into a sneer as if he were sitting in a bath with the water just a little too hot.

"What is this prison?" he remarks. "It's horrible!"

"It's an office, Thor, where people come to work. Most are not this nasty." I refrain from saying boring because I suppose some humans do like working in offices or there wouldn't be so many of them. Besides, I know how boring other planets are. Offices don't come anywhere close to it.

"Is this your office?"

"By Odin's chair, no." At least not for very long, I add to myself. I don't say it aloud and open the remark to questions from my brother. There's only so much misery one can inflict on oneself willingly. "The person you were going to have a nice venison meal with works here. I was coming to send them home. Now, dear brother, we're no longer in space and cold, so mind telling me what it was that you were doing? Why were you involved in my case?"

Thor mutters something under his breath and even as keen as my ears are, I don't hear what he says.

"Speak up, Thor," I say, again trying to imitate Frigga as best as I can.

"He's working on something for me." It's still garbled slightly, but I can make out what he's saying clearly enough.

"What's he making for you?" I wonder if there is any answer which Thor can give which might soothe my rising irritation. I frankly doubt it.

"My Aesir brothers," a calm voice says behind us, "if I might step in here."

Suddenly, this windowless and poorly aged office feels extremely small as we turn to see that Frey has joined us. I'm nearly claustrophobic as I sway on my heels and wish I could make myself feel slimmer. Here's a hint: I'm tiny for a frost giant, but frost giants never feel slim. Even as a female. Now, put me in a furniture-filled enclosed room with two muscular men and watch me scream. My only consolation is that if I feel this way, I can only image what Frey, who is used to being out in the open air nearly all the time, feels like.

Frey takes the spear from me and removes the heart of the comet from the tip. I'd been so stunned that Thor had delivered us back to this factory office, that I'd practically forgotten about that beating heart who was traversing galaxies to get to me. Fortunately, Frey hadn't.

The oval shape, though it fits in his palm, is anything but smooth like an egg. Rather, it has all these jagged edges like hoar frost prickling out from it. A fine set of leather gloves, not quite as large as those he uses for falconry, comes to his hands, protecting him from the chilling ice. He glances to me, and, when he sees that I am watching him, he sends me a small smile which also sparkles from his green eyes. Yes, he's admitting that it's a little cold for him.

"Loki, it is time for you to put the spear back together," Frey says.

"I didn't break it into four pieces." Oh, my self! Did I just hear a whine in my voice? It so sounded just like my younger self defending my person against another's accusations. Why is it that being here with Thor and Frey makes me feel like I'm still the immature trickster god unable to handle the mischief I caused, in a time long before I could accept credit for what I'd done? Before I figured out who and what I was.

"I know that. Thor did. But you need to put it back together. This has been your journey, not his," Frey tells me.

Suddenly, I'm very skeptical. Is this a test? Are they trying to find out if I have my magic back? Long story, but I am still supposed to be pretending to be under Odin's banishment. Do they know the truth, or are they just guessing? I must assume that Odin and Thor have spoken over this, but what of Frey? Gentle Frey. He and I are more akin to brothers, both of us being aligned with natural elements. His soft eyes seem to hold no betrayal in them, but how can I be sure? Why do I feel this unusual distrust toward him?

"What journey would that be?" I ask, trying not to rush the question so that I sound clueless rather than suspicious.

Frey raises his head slightly, turning, so that his slender braids of beard whisper along his tan tunic as if they were hushing me. "Thor, what was the transdimensional crafting for you and that you wish to get before Loki sends him back to his home?"

Gods, this office is getting to me. I circle round behind the desk and sit down in the uncomfortable swiveling chair. I still feel stifled behind the desk and have to peer at the other two over the monitors, but it gives me some mild comfort from the temperature rising in here.

Thor looks none too pleased. "Horns. I was having him make metal horns for my goats."

Well, I did say it before. Thor has a thing for horns.

"It's not funny," Thor says, slamming a fist against one the of the metal filing cabinets. "Do you know how they feel when they come back and they only have these little nubs on their heads? It's embarrassing for them!"

He did this for his goats' mental health? "Can't have our goats feeling lesser than other goats?" I ask, half under my breath.

"They really are quite exquisite," Frey adds. "You might have to send him home, but he is a master craftsman. It's a shame really."

"He's a nuisance to this world," I remind them as if informing them of my job. "He could have come and settled in, kept his head down, but he chose to steal life energy from children."

It is as I finish this latest dialogue that I see the bigger picture and realize now why Frey has inserted himself into this venture. I point a long index finger at him, feeling sublimely impressed at the manicured polish of my fingernail. I managed a space escapade without breaking a fingernail. I swear, women have superpowers.

"You knew Thor was right: the fawn should have popped back to life just like his goats because you willed it so. When Sif got distressed about the loss of the fawn, you came running to fix things. You knew the transdimensional had taken the life energy needed to resurrect the fawn," I say.

Then Frey did something which is very unlike him. All the kindness falls out of Frey's vivid green eyes and the gentle strength he usually possesses hardens to granite. There comes a fierceness to Frey that typically only his opponents, of which there aren't many, see.

"Put the spear back together, Loki," he says. "It's why you're here."

CHAPTER 21

Once again, and though I thought I was done, my heels sink into hot sandy ground. Sagebrush surrounds me for as far as I can see, which is much further than a human could unless they were twenty feet up in the air.

The sagebrush man, Shat'tow, shimmies up to me in that crouched, knees up-butt down, crab walk that he has. The green paint on his face looks as if he's refreshed it because the cracks in it haven't gotten deep enough to expose the black skin beneath. His brown eyes still seem the youngest thing about him, at least until he smiles and it seems to bring him to life.

"Back again without your other half," Shat'tow says.

I glance down at the spot where I, or maybe I should be saying my male essence, had been tied down in the sun. The stakes and tethers are still there, but the spot lies empty.

"Am I still not whole again?" I ask Shat'tow.

The sagebrush shrugs. He thinks for a moment. "Maybe like spear… many pieces."

"Why does everyone want me to put this spear back together?" Maybe my wise companion will have answers for me since no one else has. "What is it about this spear?"

Shat'tow looks out over the sagebrush desert. From his vantage point, there is no way that he can see very far at all. Every surrounding plant would block his sight. But he acts as if that's not the case and that he can see not only the vast landscape around him but into others worlds as well. Not for the first time, I feel strangely odd in his presence. It's not an unfamiliar feeling though as I ruminate on the sensation. No, rather it's a lot like being around Frey and his sister, Freya.

"I think," Shat'tow begins with careful slowness, "that the spear is like you in many ways. You have come to pieces. All along, you thought you were whole, but really you leave parts of you behind, never realizing you've left them."

Is this what it's like to get chilled to the bone?

"Think on this: You were born Loki of Jotunheim," Shat'tow says as he touches both the green and blue spears, "and then you were Loki of Asgard." Now he touches the black and white spears.

He has run out of spears to touch and I see his spindly fingers reaching toward me. "And you have become Loki of Midgard."

Both his hands touch me and as much as I wish to pull away, I cannot. It is clear that I am only half full of myself as I feel only one of his hands set ever so gingerly on me even though I clearly see both. Each time, he has indicated two and yet clearly the male portion of me is missing from this situation. I won't be able to put the spear back together as it takes all the pieces to go back together. If I am not whole, how can I make anything else whole.

"How very Zen of you," I say, still wishing I could back

away. My tone is harsher than I feel it should be considering the enlightenment he really just gave me.

Shat'tow bows his head as he steps back. "Shat'tow does not know this Zen, but compliment taken. You could still be stuck to ground. Long way you have already come."

"I don't know how to put the spear back together." It's a hard admission for me to make. I am a trickster god. It's always been more about me shattering the secure known to shake up people's lives. Mischief isn't about keeping the status quo. While I've had to rectify some things in the past, it's never been a chore like this. I am at a loss.

"Then I guess you should be figuring that out first."

"Yeah? I have people for that for me."

"Don't look like they here."

"That's my point," I say. "That being the case, you're going to have to help me out a bit."

"Shat'tow isn't your people either."

I give him my best coy smile. "But Shat'tow is my friend, right?"

Shat'tow grins and the sight of his happy little face brightens me up even more. I realize that I've skated dangerously close to activating the snake venom curse because I was trying to deceive him into helping me. If I'd triggered it, it would have been all my own doing. Since I didn't, maybe I should take this as one positive against all the times that it prematurely fires.

The sagebrush man shrugs. "Might be Loki's friend, but Shat'tow don't know how to put spear together either."

Well, there went that hope. Maybe the curse didn't trigger because there was no way that Shat'tow could even help me. Might be something for me to make note of.

"Not even a guess?" I ask, still hopeful.

He shakes his head and the sagebrush branches quiver in unison.

I take one last gaze around, seeing nothing but sagebrush and this spot where my masculine self had been tied down. And Shat'tow as if he were the king of the sagebrush. "Shat'-tow, what do you do here? Are you by yourself or are there others?"

"Shat'tow is here when needed."

"You were here to guard him," I say pointing to the spot where my male counterpart had been tied. " But why are you here now?"

"Still needed, I guess."

I feel as if a nerve is dancing in my back, a subtle warning that something just isn't quite right and that I should heed the intuition. It makes me feel fidgety and I fight to control it.

"Who brought you here, or who gave you the task to remain here?" I ask.

"I am here, and then I am not."

I nod that I understand. He's a spirit guardian, plain and clear. He probably doesn't know who originally brought him forth into this realm or how he comes to be until he is needed, just as he said.

"So why am I here?" I ask. Since I'm not looking at Shat'tow when I speak the question, I don't know if I'm asking him or posing it to the fabric of this realm. It feels like Midgard, but is clearly not Earth of Midgard. Probably one of the desolate planets.

But one with a guardian. And, one that had my male self held prisoner.

I do admit that I am clearly baffled.

Then Shat'tow stands up, rising to his full height which actually towers above me in heels.

"Hi," I say a little too spryly. I take a step back wondering if I'm about to be captured and tethered in the sand now. Perhaps I should have listened to that foreboding feeling. I prepare to cast several illusions of myself and move quickly should the sagebrush man try to grab me.

"Why is anyone anywhere?" Shat'tow asks, his voice much deeper than it had been previously. "Why exist?"

It was one thing for Frey to be all philosophical with me, but I couldn't believe I was going to be on this quest with Shat'tow as well.

But perhaps the two are connected. Frey is very grounded, connected to all the realms as if he were a part of the Yaggstrasil Tree itself. If Shat'tow is a spirit guardian for this world, then Shat'tow would be connected to the Yaggstrasil Tree as well.

Would that be so different than how I have connected my energy to Midgard?

"Ah," Shat'tow says. "I believe you begin to see."

He calmly takes the white and black spears from me, leaving me with the light blue and sage green ones. I bring them together and wrap my fingers around both their shafts. Closing my eyes, I feel through the fabric of Midgard that these two spears are connected. In the next moment, I am no longer holding two spears. I am holding one.

Shat'tow returns the white and black spears to me. "Now you see why you are here."

I am here because I am connected to everything.

CHAPTER 22

I return to Rhetallia's hall where her Amazons are once again training on the marble floor amid the Grecian style columns. Several of the older women sit lined out on the raised platform, watching the combatants, but they don't appear shocked to see me suddenly appear before them. Rhetallia's warriors continue with their parries and strikes without ever hitting me either, but I can feel each of them moving around me and adjusting for my presence.

Now, if this is the connection which Odin goes on about, I can see why he'd crave it, why he'd walk among the humans of Midgard in such a vulnerable fashion.

Right now, I have connection with the Amazons on a feminine level too. We are warrior sisters together. The level of power running through me sizzles. I long to join in (don't let Thor hear me think that!), but I have other work to do. I'm here for another purpose.

I hold three spears: the black, white, and the merged green and blue. As I stand there, eyes closed, in the center of the room, I bring all three together, open myself to their energy, and press them together as one.

Feeling the spear becoming a single cylinder in my hands, I hear a collective war cry issue from the women around me and all the sounds of their practice battles halt.

A surge of energy passes through me, and with a start, I open my eyes. The strange hieroglyphics on the wall which are not quite Egyptian nor Aztec begin to glow in vivid gold. Ghosts of the symbols rise in whitish blue and drift through the air, among the surrounding Amazons who stare in amazement. Slowly, the symbols glide their way toward the spear. Coming into its vicinity, the writing sucks into the shaft. For a moment, their imprint remains before dissolving into the weapon.

The Amazons move aside, giving me an aisle to walk down toward Rhetallia. I feel their eyes upon me. I wonder how many of them have been informed that the one introduced to them as Laufey when I announced it is truly the Trickster Loki.

But it is for the one with the golden hair that I made such a bold proclamation and who I hope doesn't learn my secret. It is her gaze that I seek out so I can look into her sky blue eyes and for myself if she knows the truth.

She holds no recognition toward me other than what we have already shared in my loops.

Clear disappointment runs through me and I can't believe how much that emotion wrecks me. I must shove it down so that it doesn't run through me uncontrolled enough for Rhetallia to pick up on. The leader of the Amazons does know the truth and she will pick up on my weakness. And a weakness it is to feel for someone beyond your reach. I know this all too well, and I will not have Gelsh used as a pawn against me now or in the future.

"Leader Rhetallia," I say, forcing my voice to be steady. "I return the spear to you."

With that, I practically thrust it toward her, ready to be done and away from Gelsh's soft stare. Why am I shaking? I see it in my hands, vibrating through the weapon's shaft, and feel it in my quivering high heel shoes.

"Thank you, Laufey," Rhetallia says rather loudly. It almost sounds like a reminder to me and all the other Amazons that I'd been going under a false name. Then she steps a little closer to me and leans in so she can whisper practically in my ear. "She will be returned when she is ready, Loki."

I feel as if a pole of ice had just formed in the center of my chest to immobilize me. I can't even turn my head. Only my eyes are capable of action, and I watch Rhetallia as she moves back, her gaze touching mine ever so briefly. She raises the spear into the air above her head before giving a victorious cry, which the Amazons around me repeat.

My hand is touched by long fingers and I practically jump. I glance down to see Shat'tow crouched beside me. The female warriors nearby seem to take no notice of the sagebrush man.

"Ready?" he asks.

"For what?"

"To go home," he answers.

The spear is here. Gelsh will stay to train. My other half is free from his tethers and has gone, hopefully, back home. I can see no reason to stay. Will I be back in the office at the factory, or somewhere else? If it's the office, will Thor and Frey be there?

Shat'tow firms up his grip. I can feel his wrinkled flesh now against my skin. So old and frail, yet so warm from long days under the desert sun.

I nod at him. It's time.

But Shat'tow shakes his head and tsks as he slowly lowers his head. "You still don't understand why you're here."

"Then tell me," I demand. What is this that everyone keeps going on about.

I try to pull my hand from his.

His grip is tighter than Thor's and I can feel the bones in my hand compressing.

"I thought I was here to save a fawn and bring the spear back to the Amazons," I say. Realizing I've raised my voice, I look to see if Rhetallia has taken notice. What I discover is that Shat'tow and I are now alone in the room. It might as well be as vacant as the desert.

"But why are you here?" Shat'tow asks.

I can't answer the question. I don't know what he wants to hear from me.

"Always looking to respond how people wish you to," Shat'tow says. "Think that is the correct reply. What say you?"

"I say this has been the stupidest way to have a spell triggered. A very unclever imagination."

"Now why would you say that? I thought it was quite clever." This comes not from Shat'tow but rather my male self stepping out from the shadows of one of the Grecian columns. While he could cast an illusion of himself and make him perfectly pretty as I know we usually present to the world, I see that his white hair is uneven and roughly cut. He wants to remind me that the Valkyrie have done this to him. He raises his chin ever so slightly. "Now, I ask you, why are *you* here."

He says it with such force that I feel as if I've been slapped.

As he approaches, I step back. My heels make timid little clicks on the marble floor. My heart begins to race.

"Why are you here?" he asks again.

"I'm your other half."

"Wrong. We belong together. You are not with me. You are outside of me. Why?"

I stop, realizing that I must stop defending myself against him. I need to take a stand. I suddenly realize how every woman must feel, a little meek against a male. No matter how strong, confident, or self-assured, there is always some little portion that remains skittish and like a threatened fawn when the hunter with the spear arrives.

"I am the Trickster," he says. "What are you? A part of me that wishes to mother and find connection to everything living?"

His words continue to sting.

"I am the part of you which makes you mischievous but not malicious. Without me, you go too far," I say.

"You hold me back. Imagine where I could be if I didn't have you."

"It wasn't the Valkyrie that took your hair." I realize this in a wave of a foggy memory that comes over me, right before we became two. "You cut it to separate us, to use its magic to hold us apart."

"You weren't supposed to exist outside of me. So how did this happen?" He holds out his hand to indicate me standing there before him. "Why are you here?"

This had happened on purpose. Someone had stopped Loki's plan to destroy me.

Too bad I had forgotten Shat'tow was in the room with us.

CHAPTER 23

S hat'tow's fingers once again glide against my own. The sudden reminder that he is there startles me and I momentarily take my eyes off my male self to look down at Shat'tow. His tight grey curls tangle around the sagebrush growing right out of him. He looks like a shaggy mess, but his brown eyes reflect his eagerness to be of service. What else would I expect from a spirit guide.

Like a dirty homeless man out walking through crowds hoping someone will offer him a cup of coffee. I really do think I understand Odin right now. That's a scary thought. But not quite as scary as the one that follows on its heels: this could be Odin disguised. The All-Father did favor his few daughters, making them Valkyrie. Was Odin here now, protecting me, trying to make me one of his Valkyrie and the transition failing because I am who I am and my recent troubles with the Valkyrie. The trouble is that I no longer have faith in them; they are the only ones who could play tricks on the Trickster. Never was it the other way around. Maybe it should be.

Oh, this is making my head spin.

And I was just starting to like Shat'tow too. But not if he's really Odin.

A ripple surges through the fabric of Midgard and I know this is not Odin and I must trust my guide.

Shat'tow grins, brown eyes sparkling.

Okay, let's do this.

"Siding with my captor? Do you know how long he had me tied down?" my male self asks.

"Long enough to make me angry," I answer. "What would have happened to me if he hadn't? I think I owe him a great debt."

"Well, let's get one thing straight right now." Loki's mouth tightens at the corners. "It was the Valkyrie who cut my hair, but it was an attempt to keep me from burning myself out with my magic. If they hadn't –"

There's more that he wants to say. I feel it in my chest, but I have no memory of what had brought us to such a dire moment. Why had he needed me gone? We'd always co-existed so well. Did he want Midgard for himself?

No, he wanted the heart of the comet.

But why had it come down to a choice to get rid of me so that he could possess the comet's heart?

"No more," Shat'tow growls and we vanish as I feel him yank on my arm.

We drop through time and space. I feel the rush and the unsteady landing as my heels quiver beneath me. I expect to feel the points of the shoes sink into sand, but that doesn't happen. Instead, because it's a solid surface beneath me, a jarring pain travels into my knees and hips.

"A little warning next time," I beg of Shat'tow. "I'm not as young as I used to be."

He grins, knowing that I'm mostly joking. As his hand disengages from mine, he raises it to point a crooked finger at me. "Not as old as me."

I feel the truth of his words.

A quick look around shows me that we've landed in my kitchen. We're on the far side of the island and away from the front door, though we face it as if we're expecting someone to come through it. I glance toward the living room to see if Fenrir is there stretched out on the plush white carpet. I don't see my son and I hope he's outside. If there is trouble coming through the door, I know that not only will he issue a warning bark, but he can take care of himself. One doesn't worry much about a hellhound.

"What was that about with him, the male me?" I ask Shat'-tow. "Was he real?"

"Did you sense illusion around him?" Shat'tow returns with his own query.

"No." I almost say that it scares me, but we all know that gods don't feel fear. This is truly the closest I've ever come. I think there has always been a part of me which has wondered about the day I would play a trick on myself. Am I at that day? "What happened, Shat'tow? You had him captive, so you must know what went on and how he came into your watch. It's time to tell me."

Shat'tow nods his head quickly. "Valkyrie brought him, told Shat'tow to hold him fast. They set the tethers."

I see tears enter his eyes and he breaks his gaze from mine.

"Come, we must get totem," he says.

"Not until you tell me what just upset you." I stand firm, setting my heels into the floor as if they were spikes being driven into rock. I know it's just a mental attitude rather than the real thing, but I must stand firm. There is more to Shat'-tow's story and I must hear it.

"He screamed under sun." Shat'tow stares down at the tile floor and nudges it with his foot to feel the ridges of the rock impressions as if he's intrigued by it. He might very well be since he's not used to walking on rock but rather sand. "Heat melted him."

As Shat'tow raises his head, I see the portion of his lip where he'd been chewing on while he'd been looking down and considering what to say. He's scraped it hard with his teeth. Not only is it cleaned of the green paint, but it is a little swollen as well.

It had been painful for Shat'tow to watch. Almost as painful as it had been for my male counterpart I would imagine.

"Now, you know what upset Shat'tow. Let's go get the totem." He points toward the door to the basement.

Behind the wondering of how he knew which direction to go to get the totems is a curiosity of what he thinks of the odd door with the rounded archway. I'm very proud of the crafts-manship that went into it, but what does Shat'tow think considering he has no doorways that I could see in his domain?

Perhaps his uncanny awareness of my house is because he's a spirit guide. I really don't have time to dwell.

"What totem are you after?" I'm curious myself, but I also want to discern his purpose. He hasn't said why we are here and only directed me to get the totem once we were.

"The totem of the goddess who accepted your card," he replies and his eyes reflect nothing but honesty. "She is the key to fixing you situation. You must get the Valkyrie to repair what they have done."

Is that even possible? For a Valkyrie, each hair contains a certain amount of their own magical essence. Enough that when I break it to release the magic, I can power a small spell. But Loki's hair had been cut by a Valkyrie blade. While my essence is that of the gods, I know that if I'd pulled one of my own hairs, broke it in two, I wouldn't have been able to use magic. I suppose I'd never gotten curious enough to find out if someone else could use my magic that same way.

"Many questions about how you got to this moment, but none of them serve you," Shat'tow says. "Get the totem. Not much time."

Of course. Loki would be on his way here. Would he come for the totem first or try to get ahead of me?

That spurs me to action and I go to unlock the basement door.

It's already open.

CHAPTER 24

The doorway is ancient wood, something I purchased from an old castle which was being renovated and modernized. What the new owners were throwing out, I happily collected. Then I found a brilliant craftsman to build an incredible matching archway which would make the old door feel at home here in my simple, but updated home.

The open door hadn't been perceivable from where we'd be standing in the kitchen, but as I draw close to the wooden archway, I see that the door isn't latched. It rests ever so slightly open so that even the slightest breeze could have pushed it closed. But the fact that the locking mechanisms aren't clicked together suggests – but doesn't prove – that someone is already in my basement.

Someone has come for Sif's totem. Did Loki beat me to it?

I place my hand on the wrought iron handle. I wonder who has come before me to press the tongue which would unlatch the door. I wish I could tell from a touch. I suppose the housekeeper could have unlocked it accidentally. As this door isn't very secure on its own, I have a steel door directly behind it. That has a state-of-the-art keypad keeping my basement protected against casual entry. What I find behind the open door will inform me if I have been trespassed against or not.

Shat'tow scuttles around so that he has a better view as I swing the door wide. It is his gasp that lets me know that the metal door is open.

"He's here," I mutter as I stare at the gap. I suppose I should go face him.

Shat'tow is shaking his head as he once again reaches for my hand. He wants to keep me from going down, but this is something I must do.

"Loki, is that you?" I hear Jason call out.

"Jason?" I say, but I'm speaking to Shat'tow as I say the name.

"Yes, it's me," Jason replies. "You said you couldn't get here. Did you decide to teleport on over?"

Shat'tow doesn't try to stop me this time as I head down the stairs to the basement. Maybe he'd been worried it was Loki down there too.

I see a grey shadow move across the tile as someone, presumably Jason, moves across the room. I get far enough down the stairs that I see him setting a totem on the stainless steel counter. I see from the wrinkles on back of his camel-colored suit that he's been sitting a lot today.

There's a moment where I wish I could freeze time. Of everything I can naturally turn to ice, time is not one of them. But Jason's physique in this moment strikes a very feminine part of me.

He turns, then his chocolate eyes are upon me and I see an equal interest from his appraisal and his smile. It would be so easy.

His smile fades fast. "You didn't call me, did you?"

He reaches a hand back to push the totem behind him.

"It was not I," I say.

Then he does something he doesn't often do on his own: he calls the Golden Fleece to him. I watch it drop over his shoulders just as an equally weighted sense of disappointment plummets into my gut.

Jason holds up a hand. "Loki, it's been a very confusing few months for me. Can we not do anything rash here?"

"What are you talking about?" I snap these words probably a bit too harshly. I know my male counterpart called Jason, but I don't know their conversation. If I had to guess, it was most likely something along the line of, 'If I show up as a woman, don't trust me.' How typical. I really must have a talk with myself about that attitude.

"Look, I accept a lot about you. Okay, most people wouldn't believe the things I've seen, so I get it. But you – male, female, male, female…. My head's spinning."

"Woah, you've seen me in my male form since I became a woman?" Somehow, that sentence didn't come out of my mouth like I felt it should. But what else was I supposed to say? Jason thinks it's been weird for him? Maybe he should try being me.

"I just don't need this to be a game. Let's fool Jason today; how should we show up?"

He seems really angry about this.

I finish coming down the stairs. "This isn't a game. Something's gone wrong. I've got to fix it. I can only do that with that totem."

I wish I could see what was in the totem jar. Is it really Sif's, which would be one that I haven't seen so I don't know what it is, or is it from one of the multitude of other cases I'm working on. Which one was Jason directed to retrieve?

"No," Jason says. "I'm going to take this to where the other Loki said to meet him. If you want to come along, great. Just no tricks. Got it? None. I'm not in any mood for it today."

Wow, he really is taking this badly.

"This is my house. Let's just wait here," I say as a counteroffer. "Call him. Tell him to come on home. You can even tell him I'm here if you want, just so no one thinks I'm going to lay a trap."

He eyes me suspiciously. "You mean that?"

"Why wouldn't I?"

"I… It's just been a really confusing couple of months."

"Jason, it's still me."

"Yes, but…"

"But what?"

Jason pulls a sour face, lips tight. His head gives a couple little shakes. What he's going to say to me next is very hard for him to verbalize. He doesn't even want to say the words on his mind. Finally, he gives up completely. "Never mind."

"I'm not letting you off that easily. You keep bringing it up. What has made the last couple of months confusing?" Even though I make it a demand, I don't quite put enough force into it to weave a spell.

"You…" He drops his gaze to the floor, even blushes a little.

Humans! If you got any cuter, we gods might explode.

He exhales a breath filled with anxious emotions. His lips tug awkwardly as he searches for the right words. I'm about to stop allowing him time when he finally chokes out, "You look like Medea."

Okay, well, that was not expected. I never imagined that he

would say that I looked like his wife. He hadn't been looking at the floor; he'd been glancing at the spot on his chest where the Fleece overlapped. While it had been a blush, it was one where anger fueled the embarrassment. The Golden Fleece that Medea, his beloved wife, had woven the very immortality spell which had kept Jason alive. The sacrifices she put into the magic to keep him alive had driven her mad.

The depths of his feelings, the glassy look to his eyes, his trembling lip, they all made me want to break the tension of the moment.

Because I'm Loki, I had to go with it.

"I can't believe you'd compare the two of us. I am way more stylish. I have short skirts and heels. Her toga has nothing on me."

Instead of the laugh I wanted, I got a level stare. Poor Jason. His wound ran deep. I suppose bearing that guilt for a few centuries would do that to a man.

Then his look turns into a wolfish grin. He pushes away from the counter and approaches me. "You've got that right."

CHAPTER 25

Jason stands very close in front of me and it's a very good thing that I don't need to breathe because I don't think I'd be able to stay conscious on the tight inhales I'm taking. I'm only doing that because he smells like coffee and musky cologne, that scent I get every day when he rushes in for our coffee shop meeting. There's a reason I do that. A perk that starts my day off right.

One I didn't get this morning because I was hot on the trail and leaving early to get to the factory where they make custom screws.

Here he is now, the right scent, in a suit that makes him look like a very drinkable latte, and staring at me with eyes like melted chocolate. I sense he's as hungry as I am.

"We're locked in this, you know," he says to me.

"Uh-huh," I agree mindlessly.

"Damn it, Loki. Come on, break it. Break the curse."

"Uh-huh." I put my hand on his chest, sliding fingers up beneath the Fleece. Oh, it's so warm and I can feel his heart fluttering. That damn thing isn't going to protect him from me now.

"Loki," he says. I completely miss the panic in his voice. I register it somewhere in the back of my mind, but I disregard it since I don't understand it.

His lips come to mine. Yes.

"Loki," he pleads mere seconds before his kiss deepens and we drink each other in.

"Get away from our personal assistant!"

At the sound of Loki's panicked voice and the patter of shoes on the stairs, I feel the shock snap me away from Jason. The basement which had darkened to a tunnel where only Jason existed now expands in stark whiteness from the lights overhead. I wipe my lips against my hand and I suspect that Jason does the same.

Then Loki is there. Dark suit, shiny shoes, and hair still raggedly shorn. He thrusts his way between me and Jason, standing there like an overprotective father with his hand sternly on his hip. "We have to work with that man every day."

With the extra height given to me by my high heels, I can stare directly in my own eyes. "Properness in the workplace? Is that why you separated the two of us?"

"None of this is for the reason you think," he answers.

I can hear my thoughts though I also see the truth of it in his eyes. We can't do anything that might lead to us losing Jason. Ultimately, we need him too much. He's the best dang personal assistant we've ever had, and though we joke about firing him on a near daily basis, the reality is that we want him to stay by our side forever. Best yet, Jason being who he is, that is perfectly possible. Jason really should be awarded with the *Best Personal Assistant Ever* trophy.

"Okay," I say. Loki is right and I gain my head back. "Jason said something about a curse?"

"I don't know when exactly it happened, but I suspect…" Male me huffs out a long, exasperated breath. "The transdimensional we're after … he makes things, right? Thor, well, he needed us to delay. I think he set this up."

"Thor? Are you sure? This is the guy who was having metal horns made because his goats were self-conscious about their little baby horns. I just don't see him doing something like this."

Loki turns away from me. "Well, he did."

I'm still having trouble believing it and I really dislike the way he snubbed me. Man, I am arrogant. My heels tap on the floor tile like the angry chirps of a bird as I follow him over to the totem case. It resembles a trophy case from floor to ceiling, but the glass is really solid ice. If one looks at it very closely, a frosty sheen can be noticed. Loki stands before the case, arms crossed over his chest, staring at the numerous cylindrical jars inside.

"You weren't doing a good job of taking care of business, were you?" he asks.

I could just growl or snap back, but I don't. I won't let him pull his same arrogance out of me. That's never who I've been. It's a shame he doesn't see that. Was that why he needed us separated, because I am a side of him that he would rather be without much like I don't want to possess his arrogance?

I suddenly hear Jason give an exclamation of surprise at the same time I hear Frey's voice say, "Brother, brother. Enough. Let's get the totems and be done with this already."

Totems? I latch onto the word knowing that Frey wouldn't have misspoken. He might be a free spirit, but he's not ambiguous.

Frey, friend to all spirits, goes over to Jason. He shakes one of Jason's hands while landing his other muscular hand on Jason's shoulder and squeezing slightly. I hope Frey doesn't entertain the notion of pulling the Fleece from Jason as it will never happen. While most people feel intimidated around Frey even though he'd never hurt a flea, as the saying goes, I see why Jason was once leader of the Argonauts. He meets and accepts Frey instantly as an equal. It's as if they might pop off for a beer and leave me here with myself.

Loki pivots back to the totem case and begins searching over the jars. He clearly knows what he's looking for. I cast a careful glance in the direction of Jason. I don't want to meet his gaze in case someone were to notice. I want this to seem casual, like I just happen to be waiting. I see that Jason is still in front of the totem as if he were shielding it. Now, I want to look up at his face, but I don't dare.

He called the Fleece to him for more than worrying about me.

I study his posture in my mind, trying to see what clues his stance might have given me in my brief glance. He clearly knows something more is going on. What had he said to me as we were close? There was a curse, and … what else? That I looked like his long-dead wife, Media. How long had that been going on? A couple months. He clearly said that he'd had a couple confusing months because of me.

"It's not here," Loki says. "Where is it?"

I do a casual turn toward Loki. "Which one are you looking for? I might have cleared the case already and sent the transdimensional home. I know you feel like I haven't been working, but I have."

"The heart. Where is it?"

The heart of the comet was a totem? Last I'd seen it, Frey

had the icy heart of the comet in his hands. I quickly remember that it was Thor with myself and Frey, not Loki. I was pulled away by the spell. For all I know, Frey gave the heart to Thor after I was gone.

I find Frey looking at me, not smiling, not even a quiver in the braids of his brown beard. His green eyes are not bright with their vivid color but rather darkened as if shadowed twilight covers the forest. He doesn't trust my male self either. It's one of those moments when I wish that someone had pulled me aside to let me know what was going on beforehand. Wouldn't that be nice?

On the other hand, I want to know what totem Jason is hiding. He clearly has no intention of revealing it to Loki, and Frey is still standing close enough to him that I have a delicious idea. It's hard not to smile. I spin an illusion of myself off and leave it dwelling in my current position while I move off invisible and glide behind Frey. Back-to-back, I hide behind his looming presence and make myself visible to Jason. I wonder if Frey feels me there. He does spread his stance a bit and I hear him inhale as his chest puffs up.

Jason doesn't turn, but does acknowledge me and gives a tip of his head toward the totem jar behind him as if he thought I was clueless about what I was doing here. I give him a quick nod to assure him that is the reason I am here.

I feel it, that spell coming on me.

I grab the jars, realizing now that there are two, not one. They are the reason I am here.

The spell tugs.

As I fade away, I hear Loki yell.

CHAPTER 26

I'm not surprised when the heels of my once black shoes sink into sand and I find myself surrounded by sagebrush. I am surprised by the sudden appearance of a stainless steel countertop and cabinet showing up with me. The juxtaposition of desert and metal is nearly comical.

I see Shat'tow move from around the corner of the cabinet and instantly wonder if he'd been there in my basement to teleport the cabinet with us. He grins as he squat-walks over to me.

The sun blazes down from high overhead. I wonder if it ever sets in this realm, or side dimension as I'm beginning to think of it now. It feels like Midgard, but it's not on Earth of Midgard. I'm so excited for that moment when everything returns to normal and I quit having to make these odd separations in my own thoughts. Right now, it's the only way I can see the whole expansive picture. Yet I know I'm still missing pieces.

"Totems better there than on sand." Shat'tow points his arthritis crooked finger at the totem jars then the cabinet.

I wonder if there's a reason he said that, but since I can feel the heat coming off the ground, I know he's right. I have to wonder if the sand would melt the ice that not much else would. The temperature of the stainless steel is also rising fast under the blazing sun. I give putting the jars on the sand a second thought. At least on the ground, I might be able to shade them a bit in the shadow of a sagebrush.

Shat'tow stands, his knees creaking. I don't know if I'm more unnerved by his towering above me or the fact that he's like a stretched spring. I much prefer him all compacted. However, his thin body does block the sun from reflecting off part of the countertop. I feel the near-immediate relief from the heat, so I know my jars much feel cooler as well.

He leans to look in the jars, then rests his head on his hands. "They are so pretty."

I realize I haven't yet taken a moment to look at them. One is a long, thin, white braid which looks the color of sun-bleached bone. The other is a flat, pale stone the size of my palm and which seems to be wheezing.

The braid has to be Sif's totem. I wonder if I'm once again going to be in trouble for stealing her hair. Some people just can't take a joke.

The stone resembles ice so much that I must ponder if it the heart of the comet, but why would it be a totem? Did Frey place it in the jar hoping to keep it cool? It would still not be anywhere like the cold of space. Little wonder it is wheezing. I'm not sure if Jotunheim would be cold enough for it to survive. One thing for certain though, this realm is extremely bad for it.

Yet something feels so wrong. Yes, my theory is that Frey

put the piece of the comet in the jar to keep it safe. My brain can't stop saying that it's not a totem. But it's in a totem jar, so does that make it one? Ah, frustration! It's like Schrodinger's cat; is it alive or is it dead? Is the comet a totem, or is it not?

I've rarely seen a totem be something living, and that makes my next action easy. I place my hand on the rounded end of the cylindrical cover and pull the ice back into myself. The relaxing chill that comes with it is a welcome relief from the heat.

Shat'tow leans in toward the flattened ice of the comet's heart. "You must act fast."

He's right. It's shuddering now and little flakes of its compositional makeup float off much like the tail of a comet, except these pieces give a sparkling wink as they dissolve and are gone.

"It's too hot here. I don't know that I can," I tell Shat'tow. I wish I'd left the comet heart in the case where it clearly had some cold to it. Now, the heart is just burning off fast.

"Sun good and sun dangerous," Shat'tow says. I recall him having said that to me when we'd first met.

"Yes, it is. Do you have somewhere with less sun?"

"Sun provide all. But you not tied down. Change. Make different circumstance."

If Shat'tow had been squatted down, I might have leaned over and kissed him. As it is, yes, I just need to change the circumstances. I hand the totem jar with the braid in it to him and when he takes it, he holds it against his chest with his lanky arms around it.

I lift the comet's heart off the base of the totem jar to hold in one hand while in the other I melt that base. Once it is a pool of water quickly warming on the stainless steel counter-top, I freeze the metal. With it, the water turns to ice. Setting the heart on the ice, I place both hands on the countertop and let everything freeze. Ice runs down the cabinet. The sand freezes beneath my feet. Every drop of moisture held in the air bursts into a snowflake pattern. Some I feel hit my skin. Shat'tow dances in the white dots falling around him. Through the ground, I pull ever bit of moisture I dared from the nearby sagebrush plants and breathe it into a shielding around us.

Shat'tow, with his knees coming up higher than his hips, bounces outside of the shelter while laughing. The moment his feet bury into the warm sand, I hear him sigh and mutter something about it being not so cold.

The stainless steel could become cold just as readily as it could become hot. It amplified everything I did and soon the comet heart stops quivering. The shielding I had made keeps us both out of the sun. It looks like an odd, backward C and curves around us nearly like a complete eggshell which glows from the sun beating down on the outside.

My heels are stuck in the frozen sand. A small price for the chilly relief which both the heart and I currently enjoy.

But how to keep this sensation? I couldn't exactly keep the comet heart in my freezer forever. I didn't know exactly what kind of creature this was, but I knew it was alive and that it had come to me. I had to find a way to care for it somehow. The only way that I could see how was to put it back in space.

Maybe I had just imagined that it had traversed solar systems to be with me.

I didn't even know how to ask it what it wanted. Here I was, a frost giant, and I didn't know how to talk to a creature of ice. Is this what my Jotunheim relatives foresaw in me that made them abandon me? No wonder I was like a joke to them.

Without consciously realizing what I'm doing, I pick up the

comet's heart and hold it in my palms. Will it understand me if I speak to it?

Now I admit that I am not the warmest creature out there, but in my hands the ice melts beneath the heart and once again I see it starting to fade. Before I can shout an exclamation, Shat'tow runs in and hurriedly slides the totem I had him hold onto the countertop. He then slaps my hands together. His on the outside of mine feel blazing hot as if I were in the sun. I want to make a layer of protective ice around the heart that I hold, but I can't do it with the heat coming off Shat'tow. I feel the remains of the comet dissolving.

"What are you doing?" I holler, trying to pull away from Shat'tow.

"Sometimes, you not very smart," Shat'tow says to me. "Can't hold everything same forever."

"Let go, you're killing it."

"Am I? It in your hands. Sun dangerous, but sun good."

I see that his hands are glowing around mine as if they are the sun. He has pulled down the spirit of the sun into him. In a wink of a thought, I wonder if this comet heart is dangerous. But that whisks from existence as quickly as I can feel the icy heart slipping away from between my palms. How can a child ever be dangerous? This heart is but a child's heart – light, innocent, and playful. It knew I would be a creature to understand it.

Yet, it's dying in the heat from Shat'tow.

"Spirit guide, life guide," the sagebrush man says to me. He removes his hands from the back of mine and urges me to open my palms.

I can't feel anything there anymore. There is nothing between my palms. Shat'tow seems so sure of himself, and yet,

I know it will break his heart when he realizes he's destroyed the heart of the comet.

I'm not sure if I care how Shat'tow feels.

I open my hands.

A white flame surges from my left palm. It is so cold that had anyone else been holding it at this moment, they'd be burned by the chill. As it is, I may still end up with a touch of frostbite. The flame takes a moment to stabilize and leaps to the stainless steel countertop.

Shat'tow gives a giddy little dance, but it could be the cold sand stinging his feet.

The flame opens eyes of blue and a mouth forms to take on a pleased grin. "I have found my way home."

As it stares at me and I stare back at it, I fall into a comprehension so deep I don't know how I missed it the first time. This flame had compressed so completely it had taken on the icy outer shell that would allow it a journey through space. Every bit of the protective shell had to melt away so that it could expand. But if it had done so while out in the heat of the sun, it would have faced the same fate as if the comet had flown right into that sun. It truly had needed me to catch it and bring it forth slowly, controlling its expansion back into form. As Shat'tow had said, a life guide.

"Friend safe." Shat'tow picks up the totem jar and squats back down as he hands it over to me. "Now, get hair back to you."

There's a flutter in the air as if feathers are brushing my face, and I know Valkyrie have landed.

CHAPTER 27

The heels of my shoes are still stuck in the frozen sand at my feet as I feel Valkyrie circling in around me. I step from my shoes and my feet through the silky nylons feel enjoy the feel of the cold sand.

I hear the soft flap of wings as they settle into their landing and the accompanying whisper of feathers settling in behind them.

On the stainless steel countertop, the white flame sways and its blue eyes open wide at the sight of them. I haven't yet turned to take a count of how many there are, but the flame seems in awe.

I won't let them take the flame. That's my first thought as I start to send more bitter cold through my legs to the sand. If I have to, I will make it unbearable for the Valkyrie if they step within my little shell.

Behind that goal is the thought that Shat'tow had just mentioned returning my hair to me and I realize the truth: the bone-white braid in the totem jar is my hair, that which the

Valkyrie cut from my male self. If the Valkyrie had hatched a plan to separate me into two parts – what better way to defeat a god than to half the god's powers – and they wanted to send me to another realm away from Midgard, then they had another thing coming. I would fight to stay. This was my realm now. All of it.

What if my male self didn't have the same feelings about that?

Worse, we have always been in love with the Valkyrie. There I said it. What if he's doing this for them? The more I have to endure this separation, the more I hate it. I hate not knowing what is fully in my own head and what is second guessing. My feelings for the Valkyrie aside, I will fight them if I have to.

But first, I take the totem jar with my braid inside it from Shat'tow. Only then do I turn to face the Valkyrie.

My male self steps inside the awkward shell of cool protection from the desert sun's heat. He has come with the Valkyrie. His hair is still ragged and unkempt, and his suit is beginning to take on the wrinkles of what he's been through today.

I wish I hadn't taken off my heels because I have to look up at him and see his green eyes staring back down at me. I feel beneath him, inferior.

As if to prove it, he sweeps his hand through the air and whips the domed cover off the totem jar. I feel the ice evaporate. What a cool maneuver, and I realize that he is showing me that he is much more powerful without me as part of him. Half a god's power I am not. I am less.

He takes the braid, and I don't even try to stop him.

"We are not the same," he says as if I needed to know that now. But then he leans forward. I feel the base of the totem jar vanish as the lid had. He reaches up and his fingers brush my hair back from my ear so he can whisper directly into it. "Without each other."

As he backs off, our gazes lock, and I see in his green eyes that he's hoping I will stand with him. I know myself well enough to know that everything either one of us has done has led us to this very moment. Even separated, we will work together for the good of Midgard.

The Valkyrie are looking at the white flame on the countertop. None of them have dared to enter the shell as if they are afraid to. Shat'tow, however, remains there.

Knowing the frozen sand must be hurting his bare feet, I open a little hole in the ice to let Shat'tow have only cool sand. I push the ice I'd pulled away from Shat'tow toward the rim near the Valkyrie. I doubt they'd feel the cold through their white leather, ankle high boots but that doesn't mean they won't sense the power of the frigid barrier.

Loki inches close to me. Our knuckles bump. Then he slides his fingers into mine. If I had any doubt that he would stand with me against the Valkyrie, they now vanished as quickly as he'd evaporated the ice totem jar.

Does he really have that much sway over me? Am I under his enthrall?

Of course I am.

Do I affect him the same way?

I must. Mustn't I?

His head tips toward me a little. "We're perfect together, you know?"

There's no way the Valkyrie heard him. I'm barely certain that I heard his words, but I can feel the energy – the truth – of it.

Shat'tow squat walks over to us and stretches to stand up behind us. I feel his hand come to my left shoulder, and, as if I feel a ghost of it, I know that he's put his other hand on Loki's right shoulder.

Loki looks to me and hands me the cut end of the braid where the hair is all frayed and trying to untangle. I take it in my hand.

Behind us, Shat'tow gives a giggle. "You're rubber, I'm glue. I stick us all together."

He squeezes us tightly, and, for a moment, I wonder if he's trying to physically press us together. Doesn't Shat'tow know that for us to rejoin, it's going to take some magic?

The absurdity of all this grabs me. I close my eyes, wondering what the Valkyrie must be seeing: two Loki's and an odd man with sagebrush sticking right out of him standing behind us, inside a little frozen partial shell with a stainless steel cabinet and a white white flame all in a larger desert. I had never expected this to be my adventure today. Who would have seen this coming?

Then, I feel nothing but frozen sand beneath my feet.

I open my eyes to see that my male counterpart and Shat'tow have disappeared. I no longer hold my braid in my hand.

For a moment, the Valkyrie stand like silent sentinels at the edge of the shell, but then the leader of the regiment nods to those beside her. The dismissed Valkyrie turn and open their wings to quietly fly off. I get the impression that this was not how they expected this to go down.

The hand of the remaining Valkyrie twitches at her side, and, for a moment, I expect that she's going to point a finger at me and issue a cryptic warning about how next time she'll get me and my little dog too. Instead, she gives me a closed mouth smile and a tiny nod. Her wings stretch and she takes flight straight up into the blue sky.

I realize that I'm almost alone now. It is me and the white flame. It sways in an imaginary breeze and grins happily at me. I step from the shell and stare out at the destitute landscape. I already miss Shat'tow who has always been my companion here.

And yet, I can feel him inside as a part of me. I am whole once more.

I stare back at the white flame and wonder what the purpose of it is. I suppose that for now, it just is, and I will learn its story another day.

For now, it's time to go home.

CHAPTER 28

Click. Click. Click. Click. Click.

The staccato sound of my heels on the sidewalk echo a path I have walked down before as I head toward the factory.

It feels strange to be whole and at home. I wonder how I had never realized over the last few months that I was missing a part of myself. I don't remember everything that happened, though I do have fragments. I wonder if I will ever have complete memories. Whatever my male self is hiding from me, he's hiding it well.

Right now though, I have too many cases that need to get completed, and I'm dang well going to start with this one. It has already been delayed enough. This time, it is an afternoon appointment and the sun beats down from overhead. I don't seem to notice it as much.

The grass has been freshly mowed and the aroma of it still lingers in the air. It is certainly not like the scent of sagebrush.

Heavy footsteps fall in beside me as I feel a familiar

whoosh. Thor begins walking beside me. "Please, Loki, a little more time."

No greeting, and I roll my eyes. "He needs to go home. I don't care what kind of talent he has. He can't go around stealing life energy."

"It wasn't stealing. He was tapping into it."

"Is he planning on giving it back?"

"Loki…"

"Then he's stealing. And, if you want your goats to have horns, then I suggest you not feast on them just because you're out and away from Sif's cooking. Go home. Or buy them some reindeer antlers and strap them on." Okay, I mean that last part as a joke, but Thor inhales like it's the best idea he's ever heard. He seems to be taking me seriously and thinking about it.

"Fine." Thor disappears. He's probably already starting the search for reindeer antlers. Or maybe he did realize that I was only joking and has left in a huff. Either way, I am clear to do my job.

Except that he comes back one moment later with the transdimensional dangling from one hand and holding the man off the ground. The transdimensional's arms and legs pinwheel helplessly and he sends me a pleading look as if I'm going to help him.

"Skreli farhausten kjord," I say, touching the transdimensional. For one second, I wonder if my spell will go through him and send Thor back to Asgard as well. Unfortunately, only the transdimensional disappears.

"Case closed?" Thor asks. "Do we go for a feast now?"

"Are you just hoping someone will cook for you so you don't have to eat your goats?"

"Loki."

That might as well be a yes. At least he did stop me from having to go in that terrible office again. I just don't think I could walk by that small room where the front receptionist had shoved me. The whole smell of the place might be too much for me. He did save me from having to walk in there.

I spin around, happy to be going the other direction back toward the parking lot. "Sure, Thor. I don't want you in my car though. You'd find it too small and Jason is with me. We'll meet you there."

Thor starts to walk off across the grass, but I hear him mutter in a mocking voice as he goes, "Jason's with me." Then, under his breath, "Didn't want to go in your small car anyway."

I just smile to myself and I'm still grinning when I get into the car beside Jason.

"That seemed easy," Jason says.

"Except now I have to have dinner with Thor. You're coming so I don't suffer in misery alone."

He wants to have a sarcastic quip and I see it on his face that he's having problems restraining it. But I've told him that I will answer what I can on his question, and he doesn't want to endanger that. I'm not sure how much I will know myself. Maybe he'll end up filling in some blanks for me. If not, then we also have Thor captive at dinner. This is turning up roses for me. I do like roses.

He manages to swallow the wisecrack while I fasten my seatbelt and start the car. "Do you trust Fenrir to keep an eye on the flame while we're gone to diner?"

"It seemed very pleased when I put it inside the fireplace," I say.

"You know that's an electric fireplace, don't you?"

"Exactly. It's not like the flame is hot. I just put him in like

I was changing a lightbulb. I think seeing all the sparkles he makes on the reflective, fake tinder will delight him all night. Fenrir is happy because it gives him an excuse to sleep on the couch without getting into trouble. I think it's a win/win."

Jason's serious mood deepens. "What is it and why is it here?"

"I don't know." I brake at the stop sign and look in each direction before proceeding down the road. It's a good half-an-hour to town and it'll feel longer than that if Jason stays in this somber state. "If it's devious, we'll find out soon enough. Right now, it can't move very far on its own and seems happy as can be. It came from awfully far away."

"So do the transdimensionals you send home."

"I only send them home if they are up to no good here. If that flame or whatever it is causes trouble, I'll put it on the first comet out of the solar system myself."

"I don't even want to know how you accomplish that," Jason says as he looks out the side window. "But, are you ever going back to your male self?"

"You are worrying about a lot of things." I stretch out my fingers as I make a turn and watch as the deep purple polish on my fingernails glints in the late afternoon sun. "What I want to know is why you said it had been confusing, and why you said that the plant needed to be shut down. I never quite did figure out what you meant by that, but I figured it had to do with Shat'tow."

"Shat'tow?"

"Yeah, the funny little sagebrush covered man with me at the house when I came to get the totems."

Jason shakes his head as if I've lost it. "I don't know, but that's what you told me to say." There's a pause while his look changes to one of pure confusion. "You really have no idea what you – the other half of you -- has been doing the last couple of months? I expect double pay on my checks for the next few."

"That's why I pay you a salary."

"Yes, but I thought I'd only have one boss ordering me around all hours of the day and night, not two of you."

It's exactly at that moment that I feel a presence in the back seat as Sif says, "He does have a point, Loki. I think you ought to pay the human."

Her sudden appearance is enough to make me park the car at the side of the road. I unclick the seatbelt so I can turn to face her. Before I can say anything, she says, "I owe you for getting the truth out of Thor."

"Frey had it. I didn't do anything."

"For once, Loki, take some credit for doing something right," she snaps, making Jason give a chuckle, which he quickly hides behind the guide of a cough. "I know you want answers about what happened, but Thor doesn't have them."

"Who does then?" The words are out of me before I realize that I might not want the answer.

Sif shakes her head. "I don't know. I heard Odin issue the command for the Valkyrie to follow you, and for them to put Gelsh with the Amazons, which the Valkyrie were not happy about and did unwillingly because they had to give her memories back to her. All I know is that for you to rip yourself into pieces, whatever the mission was, it had to be dangerous. If I were you, I'd stay a woman for a bit longer. The male part of you might need some time to process everything that you went through."

I hear her words, all of them, but my mind latches onto one she'd said in particular. "Soul Ripper?"

"You don't know what that white flame is yet."

I almost hear the wheels of Jason's brain turning in confusion. All I know for certain is that Sif won't say much more in the human's presence. Possibly mine too if she thinks for one moment that a Soul Ripper is involved. There is so much more to come, but she's right: for now, my masculine self needs time to heal and maybe to process some very bad things through his psyche.

"Are you hungry, Sif? We were about to meet Thor for dinner. You're welcome to join us?"

"Hmm, human food. Yes, I can be in the mood for human food today," she responds as if she's saying that she'd like to go out for Italian over Chinese.

"Great." I buckle back in and begin to drive once more. I know I'll have to face Jason's questions about the conversation later, but for now I'm going to relax and enjoy myself. Tomorrow, I can return to saving Midgard from the transdimensionals who want to come here and mess things up for the humans. That's why I'm here.

We get to the restaurant and I find a parking spot right next to Thor's chariot. I can tell no human can see it because Jason makes no comment about it or the grazing goats. It looks to be about six of them, all fine and healthy.

Jason helps Sif get out of the backseat and we all look around for Thor. We find him waiting near the door. Now he is visible to the humans, and they are giving him odd looks as they come or go through the restaurant doors.

"Loki, Sif!" he calls out as he stands up and we all see the reason he's getting odd looks. He's wearing a set of antlers. "Look reindeer horns."

Sif shakes her head and looks at me. "Thor and his horns, I swear."

I can almost feel Jason's horror at walking into the restaurant with a dinner companion wearing ridiculous antlers. Sif might be able to put up with the humor of it and not realize what the humans are thinking, but Jason will never live it down.

I flick my fingers to cast a bit of magic. "Don't worry. I have an illusion for that. Let's go eat."

THE LOKI ADVENTURES CONTINUE…

The Loki Adventures

1-800-CallLoki (Omnibus of novellas 1-5)

1-800-IceBaby

Help Wanted, Call Loki

1-800-Lok8

Dressed to the 9's

… and more coming soon.

Fenrir's Tales

School Time

Jason's Date

On Account of Rain

Red Garnet Boots

Beth Mason Adventures

Enjoy paranormal mysteries? Join Loki's "niece" as she solves mysteries that the police categorize as "unexplained."

Ring of Stars

Because you're perfect just as you are, here's a secret code for you. Use code BPERFECT10 at checkout to get 10% off any items in the Morning Sky Studios store. Books, mugs, shirts, whatever you like.

Make new discoveries. Uncover new favorites.

www.morningskystudios.com

THE FATE OF THE WORLD LIES IN HIS HANDS. BUT IS HE THE REDEEMER OR SOMETHING FAR WORSE?

PRAISE FOR TANGLED MAGIC:

"I cannot wait for the next book to find the answers. I highly recommend reading all of Ms. Blair's tales as she is masterfully crafting many universes to explore."

WWW.MORNINGSKYSTUDIOS.COM

READY FOR ANOTHER QUEST?

Sign up for Dawn Blair's newsletter to learn about new releases, hear about events, and more!

It's easy.

Go to **www.dawnblair.com/newsletter** to join the adventure.

About the Author

Dawn Blair grew up on a ranch in a rural Nevada town. The old buildings provided inspiration for her imagination as she thrived on stories of unicorns, princesses, heroic knights, and hidden doors to other dimensions.

For as long as she can remember, Dawn has had a passion for storytelling. Though she started out writing, her creative life expanded into painting and illustration.

Thank you for taking the time to join her on these adventures.

Find more about Dawn and her work at:
www.morningskystudios.com

facebook.com/dawnblairbooks
instagram.com/dawn.blair